Mama's Ring

A Novel

Mama's Ring

A Novel

Kari S. Adams

MAMA'S RING copyright © 2019 by Kari S. Adams
All rights reserved.
ISBN 978-0-578-49875-1

Cover art designed by Kari S. Adams

For Eric—no matter what

Author's Note

This novel is fictional and is not intended as a historical work. Well-known figures, events, and places are fictionalized. It is my humble tribute to the six million voiceless who were murdered and the survivors who struggled to have their voices heard.

Mama's Ring

CONTENTS

PART I. CONFRONTING EVIL

1964

Chapter 1. It Cannot Be

"*Wir müssen das Auto reparieren*, Markus."

Rose Berzon's head snapped toward the shrill voice, and terror instantly filled her body. *My mind is playing tricks. It is not possible. That cannot be her.*

"You must lower your voice and speak English, Helga."

Rose silently panicked as she drowned in her memories, which were rising like floodwaters after a spring thaw. "The car must be repaired at once!" Helga nearly shouted at her husband, the customer service manager at Dominick's Food Mart.

"I will call about the car when I finish work. Now go home; I will be there soon."

After twenty years, I recognize that beastly face. She should be in hell, Rose thought as Helga turned from the man. The women's eyes locked for no more than a second and Rose was again at Auschwitz. She could still feel Helga Küster's whip slicing the skin on her back.

"Ma'am. Ma'am? That is sixty-eight cents, ma'am."

Rose's hands shook as she fished through her coin purse to find exact change. She did not hear the bag boy thank her for shopping at Dominick's when he handed her the Polish kielbasa and cabbage in a brown paper bag. As she ran to the car, she fumbled through her purse until she heard the faint tinkle of jagged metal. The key, too, was uncooperative, and she cursed the small flakes of white paint that fell as she scratched the area around the door's lock. When the lock popped, she flung open the door, threw the groceries into the back seat, and slid behind the steering wheel.

She stared through the windshield and saw it all again. Yellow stars, children starving to death in the streets. Jacob, Anshel, Tzeitel, Mama, and Papa. She again smelled the stench belched from tall chimneys by flames that never stopped. Helga Küster, in full guard's uniform, screamed at the prisoners as she marched around camp in shiny black leather boots.

The cashier from Dominick's tapped on the car window. "Hon, are you okay?"

The movie in Rose's mind paused. "Yes, thank you."

When Rose reached home, she left the groceries in the car and ran inside. "How can that horrible woman be here?" she screamed into the kitchen.

"Mom?"

"Why are you here?"

"The game ended early. Because of the rain."

"It rained?"

"Mom, what's wrong?" Larry was twelve years old and had never seen his mother so upset—even when she talked about the camps.

"Go to your room and do your homework. Where is Alex?"

"He'll be home pretty soon. What happened, Mom?"

"I said go to your room."

Larry's eyes filled with tears.

"Now!"

Rose leaned against the counter, closed her eyes, and let the movie of her past start again. The shot was of Szeroka Street. It was late in the day and the camera zoomed in on Papa's bookstore. Her grandfather opened the door with a big smile and lifted a little girl in his arms. After forty years, Rose still felt his whiskers tickling her face.

The lights in the bookstore went out and Papa appeared. He carefully locked the door, took little Rose into his arms, and playfully kissed the end of her nose. She giggled.

"We have to hurry, we cannot be late for supper." Papa did a silly imitation of Mama when she became angry. Little Rose giggled again. She was a happy girl; she did not know about evil. Not yet.

The bang from the screen door stopped the movie again.

"I have told you to open doors like a human being, Alex."

Barely eleven and Rose's youngest child, he was stunned by his mother's sharp tone. He slowly placed his baseball bat and glove on the floor and stooped to untie his cleats.

"Idź do swojego pokoju."

He started to cry. "I don't understand Polish, Mom."

"That is no excuse. Get up to your room and do not come back until I call you. Go."

The brothers, too confused and scared to speak, waited in Larry's bedroom.

Rose sat at the Formica kitchen table. The movie picked up where it had left off, and she watched until her husband burst into the house.

She and Samuel had married in a displaced persons camp after the war. Both of their families, including their spouses and children, were murdered by the Germans: hers in Kraków and his in the Polish countryside. The couple still wondered if it was a blessing or a curse that their families were spared from Auschwitz.

Samuel dropped his briefcase and hat on the counter. "Rose, what is the matter?"

"Why are you home so early? It is just four o'clock."

"Larry called and said something is wrong." He sat next to her and held her hands. "What is it?"

"She cannot have followed me here."

"Who, Rose?"

"It is impossible. They never would have let her in. Did she pick Skokie because of the number of survivors who live here? Is she just . . . "

"Rose, I do not know what you are talking about."

"Helga Küster."

"Are you certain? There are many Germans who came to the United States."

"I am positive, Samuel. That beast lives here. I was at the grocery store, and I heard someone shouting in German. When she turned around, she looked right at me. I would recognize those eyes anywhere."

"Did you speak to her?"

"We must, Samuel. We have no choice. If she is here, there are more."

"Rose, we cannot leave Skokie. What about the boys' school? And my business?"

"To hell with all of that. I am not going to let my family be murdered again. We must leave here at once."

Samuel simply held his wife's hands. He was reminded of his little shtetl in Poland, where, in 1940, the Germans arrived to clear the entire region of Jews. He'd lived on the farm his family had owned for three generations. In January, soldiers had forced him, his wife, and six children into a canvas-covered truck for what was called, "resettlement." He'd fought, but the two hundred pounds of muscle built during a lifetime of hard work was no match for the soldiers. A rifle butt had hit his lower back, and he'd fallen into the dirt. His oldest son, not yet thirteen, had been forced to lift his father into the truck.

At the Jewish ghetto in Lublin, the family had jumped off the truck and blended into the overcrowded streets where hunger, disease and death was simply part of life, but at least his family had been together. A few weeks later, he'd been among thousands of men who were forcibly marched to Bełżec concentration camp. Through luck and sheer will, he'd survived.

After the war, he went back to Lublin where he learned that his wife and children had been sent to Treblinka.

"We must go to the police. They will deport her."

Rose slumped back into her chair, defeated. "Do you think the police give a damn about a guard from Auschwitz?"

"I do not know, but we cannot just pretend she is not living under our noses."

"It does not matter. I will never go back to that grocery store."

"What if we see her at a restaurant? Do we politely ask her to join us?" He reached for the telephone receiver on the wall. "No, I am calling the police."

"Please, Samuel, I cannot talk to strangers about this. It probably is not her."

"If you believe you recognized her, Rose, then it is her. Tell me exactly what happened."

"Samuel, I think the man was her husband. Helga Küster is married and I do not know her husband's name." Rose put her head in her hands.

"It will be easy to find out the man's name." He pulled a thick telephone book from a drawer and opened the yellow pages to "Grocery Stores". "You said it was the Dominick's?" Samuel called the store and a man with a thick German accent answered.

"Thank you for calling Dominick's. This is Markus Roth. How may I assist you?"

Samuel's stomach dropped when he heard the man speak. "Would you please repeat your name, sir?"

"My name is Markus Roth and I am the customer service manager. How may I assist you?"

Samuel slowly hung up the telephone. "Rose, her name is now Helga Roth." He found the number for the police department. "Hello, this is not an emergency. I need to speak to someone concerning a criminal. No, sir, the crime was not today. It was many years ago in Poland. Yes, sir, I understand. Perhaps we can speak with someone else." He scribbled on a pad of paper next to the telephone. "Yes, I will contact the INS. Thank you, sir. You have been a great help."

"What did he say?"

"There is nothing the police can do, but maybe the US Immigration and Naturalization Service can help."

Rose touched the ring finger on her right hand. Mama's ring was all that was left of her life in Poland. "Yes, this time we will fight."

That night, when Samuel's breathing was steady, Rose slipped on her robe and pulled two suitcases from under the bed. She quietly opened the latches and counted four winter coats and four pairs of warm, thick-soled shoes. When the boys were little, the suitcases had held diapers, baby clothes, and small toys. Every year, she replaced the contents with larger clothes and shoes, replaced toys with books and puzzles, to keep the boys busy and quiet, in case they were in hiding. Currency of every denomination was tucked into the pockets of both suitcases. She and Samuel had saved every penny they could until they had $5,000, enough to flee.

She closed the latches and slid the suitcases back under the bed. A blanket and pillow waited for her on the top shelf of the closet, and she carried them to the front room, where she opened the drapes just enough to see a cone-shaped glow illuminating the street. She tightened the belt on her chenille robe, leaned against the pillow she'd arranged against the back of the old-fashioned rocking chair, covered her lap with her blanket, and waited. She was determined that no soldier would wake her and her family in the middle of the night ever again.

ങ്ങരുങ്ങരുങ്ങരു

Helga Roth leaned over the turntable and carefully placed the needle on the edge of the spinning album. The first note of *Ride of the Valkyries* was a warm kiss from her beloved, long-lost life, and it transported her to Nuremberg. She was in the schoolroom where the teacher's enthusiasm for the Thousand-Year Reich captivated her. She blushed at her childish naïveté, recalling the time she believed she could convince her parents, Fredderecke and Cäcilia Küster, to join the Party. But they never did understand the Führer.

Next, her throat tightened when she remembered the day she was denied leadership of a *Bund Deutscher Mädel* group, the female arm of the Hitler Youth. It was her dream that she would first have the most highly decorated BDM group in Nuremberg, then in Bavaria, and then in all the Fatherland.

In Helga's memory, she was sixteen years old again, dressed in her BDM uniform, with her long braids bouncing against her back as she thrust her right arm into the air, shouting, "Heil Hitler!" with two hundred thousand others at Zeppelin Field. The bravest men in the Reich goose-stepped before the Führer as he solemnly held the traditional stiff-armed Nazi salute, an honor reserved for the tens of thousands of men who pledged their lives to him.

The Führer's favorite piece of music soared, and she became giddy with the same anticipation she had felt in September 1939, when she'd joined the war effort. Not content to work in a factory, she'd answered a help wanted advertisement in the *Nürnberger Zeitung* on a whim and had been accepted into the concentration camp guard training program. Years had not diminished her memories of Ravensbrück, and she clearly saw the girl who refused to beat a prisoner beg as she was dragged inside the fence. The faces of each woman in the first class she'd trained were still dear to her heart. But the most wonderful days of her life were at Auschwitz.

She drifted back to her boyfriend, Günther, when they were on holiday at the SS resort near Auschwitz, and she saw the girls on the men's shoulders, taking turns being "it" while they shouted, "Marco Polo!" in the Soła River, south of the dock where trucks dumped the ashes from the camp's crematorium. They had never been bothered when the wind was just right and they could smell the camp.

The time she had broken her finger while whipping a prisoner was probably the clearest memory of all. She had continued despite the pain—a demonstration of her true strength.

When the scratching sound of the phonograph needle against the record label made her realize she was in America in 1964, her heart broke—the good old days were only a memory.

Chapter 2. The INS

Samuel watched the second hand on the smiling chicken clock in the kitchen slowly tick. He took a sip of his black coffee and felt relieved Rose did not cancel the appointment with the Immigration and Naturalization Service even though part of him had hoped she would.

"Well? What do you think?"

He looked up from his cup. "You look wonderful, Rose. Are you sure about this?"

"It would be impolite to cancel now. Let us go."

He cautiously merged the car onto the expressway and inched along with Chicago's morning rush hour traffic. Tempers flared, and car horns blew nonstop, as if the noise would make the cars move. Samuel tuned the car radio to WGN, and the weatherman promised the day would be sunny and mild. He heard the words, but suddenly he could not understand English. The traffic finally started to move, and soon Samuel exited the expressway at Congress Street.

In front of the nondescript government building, "No Parking" signs kept the street clear and sent drivers to a parking garage two blocks away. Samuel pulled into the garage and parked in the first open space. "We must hurry; we should not be late."

Rose and Samuel walked quickly to the government building and were dazzled. The elaborate lobby was decorated with bold colors that zigzagged around huge stained glass windows. Murals painted by artists commissioned by the Works Progress Administration during the Depression, captured the essence of the city. One depicted the stockyards at the turn of the century, replete with cattle in chutes on their way to slaughter. The opposite mural showed burly men as they poured steel and shielded themselves from the heat.

At the information desk, Samuel cleared his throat to get the attention of a young woman in a gray uniform.

She lifted her head out of a romance novel. "Can I help you?"

Rose unfolded a white linen sheet of writing paper with the immigration officer's name and the scheduled appointment time handwritten in her neat, European-style letters. "Excuse me, we have an appointment with an immigration officer, Mr. Hugh O'Doyle. Can you tell us where his office is?"

The clerk pointed to the elevator bank. "Take the elevator to the third floor. Look for suite three-two-seven. You can't miss it."

Samuel led Rose into the elevator and pushed the "Up" button.

"I cannot do this, Samuel. I do not know what to say."

"Yes"—Samuel squeezed her hand—"you can . . ."

The elevator doors slid open, and a white arrow on the wall pointed to the right for suites 300 to 327. They turned right and stopped at the end of the hallway at a door that had "US Immigration and Naturalization Service, Investigation Division" painted in black letters on frosted glass. Samuel pushed open the door, and the middle-aged secretary behind the desk stopped typing. Her nameplate said "Louise Davis," and she had a kind face with deep wrinkles around her eyes and lips. Her teeth were yellowed, as if she'd smoked three packs a day for twenty years.

"Pardon me. My name is Rose Berzon, and this is my husband, Samuel. We have a ten o'clock appointment with Mr. O'Doyle."

"I'll tell him you are here." Louise balanced a burning cigarette on the edge of an ashtray already full of half-smoked butts, and left her desk. The cigarette's cherry melted the paper on another butt, and Rose snuffed out both cigarettes.

A few minutes later, Louise reappeared and ushered Rose and Samuel into O'Doyle's office.

Hugh O'Doyle stood up and motioned to the chairs in front of his desk. "Please, make yourselves comfortable. What can I do for you, Mr. and Mrs. Berzon?"

Rose studied the crow's feet around his green eyes and his graying moustache. "Forgive me for asking such a question, Mr. O'Doyle, but did you serve in the army during the war?"

"The Navy drafted me in '42 and sent me to the Pacific. Why do you ask?"

"I had hoped you served in Europe."

"Mrs. Berzon, don't worry, I was doing this job before the war and luckily, my job was waiting for me when I got home. So, I have a lot of experience; there isn't anything that I haven't heard. Please, tell me how I can help."

Rose's fingers tightened around her purse and drew a deep breath. "I saw a woman I knew in Poland during the war at my local grocery store. She was a guard at Auschwitz."

"A guard at Auschwitz?" He tapped a pencil on his desk. "I have to admit this is the first time I've heard a report about a Nazi. Mrs. Berzon, are you sure you aren't mistaken?"

"No, Mr. O'Doyle, I am not mistaken. I will never forget that voice or those eyes."

"Was she stealing from the store or something like that?"

"Mr. O'Doyle"—Rose dug Mama's ring into her palm—"I saw this woman do unspeakable things at Auschwitz. Is that not enough?"

"I would really like to help, Mrs. Berzon, honest. I know all about what the Nazis did, but there is nothing the INS can do unless she broke the law in the United States. Did you see her doing anything illegal? Did she park in front of a fire hydrant or get a speeding ticket?"

"No, Mr. O'Doyle. I saw her do nothing illegal here."

"I can't go after someone, even a Nazi, if they haven't broken any laws in the US. Unfortunately, my hands are tied. You do understand, don't you, Mrs. Berzon?"

Rose fought back tears. "Thank you, Mr. O'Doyle. I am very sorry to have bothered you."

Chapter 3. Old Friends

Thursday was Helga's favorite day of the week because it was when her closest friends joined her and Markus for the evening. There were two couples and two single men, all Germans. Helga had met the wives in church when they volunteered to bake for the annual church picnic, and Markus had met the two single men at a local bar that was supposed to resemble a German beer hall. The friendships grew strong over the years through their shared interest in the past.

Helga woke early and cleaned her house from top to bottom, then baked her famous strudel. By noon, her kitchen was clean, and she had stacked dishes and silverware for her guests on the buffet in her dining room.

After lunch, she closed all the curtains in the house and climbed the attic stairs. One by one she took down three unmarked boxes and carefully placed them on the coffee table in the front room. Then she pushed the attic stairs into the ceiling, retrieved the step stool from under the kitchen sink and placed it against the wall to the left of the front door. She slid a rolled up red cloth out of the largest box and climbed onto the step stool.

She hooked the cloth's braided cord to two nails Markus had pounded into the wall years before, let the six-foot-tall banner unfurl downward, climbed off the step stool, and did the same thing to the right of the door with an identical banner. Finally, she hung a large flag on the curtains that covered the plate glass window facing the street. Helga stood back and admired her work. *How I miss seeing these every day*, she thought as she smoothed the white disk and black swastika on the flag and the banners. *The Führer would be so proud.*

The second box was filled with framed pictures of Hitler. She blew imaginary dust off the small ones as she stood the frames on end tables in the front room, next to the dishes and silverware on the buffet, and on her kitchen counter. On a shelf below the medicine cabinet in the guest bath, she gently placed an oval, gold-plated frame holding a color picture of the Führer in full uniform.

Helga returned to the front room and gently pulled a large, ornate dark mahogany frame from the box. The man in the picture stared straight through her and belonged in the center of the dining room table where she,

Markus, and their guests would gather to honor him with a *"Heil Hitler"* and a one-armed salute.

The last box contained her most precious possession—a china plate with a slight crack in the rim near the swastika. Markus had presented her with the plate for their tenth wedding anniversary, and every Thursday, she displayed the plate in the shadow of the Führer.

By seven thirty that evening, their guests had made themselves comfortable on the sofa and side chairs, and Markus turned two dining room chairs toward the front room for himself and his wife. Helga served coffee and strudel to her guests and then sat down next to her husband.

There was the usual small talk until Markus asked her a question that was on everyone's mind. "Have you seen that Jew again?"

Some weeks before, Helga had told the group about someone she noticed when she went to see Markus at the grocery store. She could not be sure, but she thought it was a Jew she had known while she was in Poland during the war. But there was no way to be certain.

"We have discussed that Jew far too often, Markus." Helga said.

Johanna, who had emigrated to the United States with her husband, Albert, a former Luftwaffe officer, said, "Helga, we are all in danger because of your Jew."

"I will not talk about this any further. It is time to begin." Helga opened her worn copy of *Mein Kampf* and read one of her favorite passages aloud. "The Führer writes: 'The black-haired Jewish youth lies in wait for hours on end, satanically glaring at and spying on the unsuspicious girl whom he plans to seduce, adulterating her blood and removing her from the bosom of her own people. The Jew uses every possible means to undermine the racial foundations of a subjugated people.'"

"Helga, you cannot simply change the subject. If a Jew did recognize you, we are all in a terrible position."

"I told you to keep silent, Johanna. Who cares what some Jew thinks?"

"How can you be so sure?"

"Because the Führer was right about the Jews; they are rats, poised to infect the entire world with their diseases." Helga rose to address the entire assemblage. "You see, my dear friends, it matters not if this Jew bitch does try to make trouble for me. There is no one in the United States of America who gives a damn about the Jews or the Nazis. Would anyone like more coffee?"

Chapter 4. A Feeling

Raindrops fell from O'Doyle's umbrella as he balanced it against the perfectly shaped stain behind his office door. He shook off his raincoat and hung it on a coat-tree and then did the same with his panama hat. The weather forecast that morning had promised occasional light showers all day, so he had left his galoshes at home. He had believed the weatherman on the radio and had paid for it with wet socks all afternoon.

He scooted himself under his desk and drummed his fingers on the arms of his rolling chair. "Louise, get Mrs. Rose Berzon on the phone. She was the lady with her husband last week—the Polish lady."

A simultaneous flash and loud boom got his attention. He looked at the rain-obscured view of the Chicago skyline. His desk used to face away from the window, but his experience as a tail gunner on B24s left him squeamish about being approached from behind.

Louise searched through a messy stack of papers on her desk. Every New Year's Day her only resolution was to keep up with her filing and every year she forgot the resolution by February. When she found the Berzon appointment sheet near the middle of the stack, she picked up the telephone receiver and dialed the number on the top line. A female voice answered on the third ring. "Mrs. Berzon? This is Louise at the US Immigration Office. Please hold for Mr. O'Doyle." She placed the call on hold. "Mr. O'Doyle, I have Mrs. Berzon on line one."

O'Doyle grabbed a pad of paper and a pencil and picked up his receiver. "Mrs. Berzon, thank you for taking my call."

"How can I help you, Mr. O'Doyle?"

"I have been thinking about our conversation. It seems to me that if you saw someone you knew who was a guard at Auschwitz, the question becomes, how did this person get into the country? If she's a citizen, she had to fill out a whole lot of paperwork, and well, there were a lot of questions that she might not have wanted to answer."

"What do you mean, Mr. O'Doyle?"

"If, and it's a big 'if,' this woman filled out an application to get into the US, she would have had to swear that she was never a member of the Nazi party or that she hated Hitler, stuff like that. So I'm thinking, *if* she filled out an immigration application and *if* we can find it and *if* she lied on it and *if* we can prove she lied, we might have a case to deport her, but like I said, Mrs. Berzon, a lot of things have to come together."

"What do you need from me?"

"I just need her name."

"Helga Küster. K-Ü-S-T-E-R. The *u* has an umlaut."

O'Doyle noted the letters. "What is an 'umlaut'? Is that those dots over the *u*?"

"Yes, Mr. O'Doyle. But her name may have been Americanized and spelled K-U-E-S-T-E-R."

"That's perfect." He hoped Rose did not catch his slightly sarcastic tone.

"Mr. O'Doyle, that was her maiden name. Her husband's name is Markus Roth. M-A-R-K-U-S R-O-T-H. I do not know when she was married."

"Got it. Mrs. Berzon, I have to warn you that this is a million-to-one shot, and it'll take a while, but I'll try."

"Why do you now believe you can help, Mr. O'Doyle?"

"I'll tell ya. I was stationed in the Pacific, but word got around about the Nazis. Thanks, again, Mrs. Berzon. I'll be in touch."

Another flash outside his window caught him by surprise. He instinctively searched for Jap Zeros over Lake Michigan. In his mind, he was twenty-five thousand feet in the air, freezing his ass off, his gloved hands squeezing Carmen's trigger. He had named the fifty-caliber machine gun after the Brazilian bombshell, Carmen Miranda; both of their swivels kept him awake nights. When he was satisfied there were no Zeros over the lake, he sat down and thought about how he would find Helga Küster Roth.

"Louise, get me Atlanta."

"Atlanta, line one."

In one motion, he picked up the receiver and pushed down the flashing square button. "Who am I speaking to?"

"Hanson, archives supervisor."

"This is O'Doyle from investigations in Chicago. I need an application."

"Name and date of application."

"Helga Küster Roth. I don't have the date. Oh, yeah, the name Küster might have those Kraut dots over the *u* or might be spelled with *ue*."

"If you aren't sure of the spelling, how do you expect me to find the application?"

"I'm sure you will figure it out, Hanson."

"Country and city of application."

"Maybe Germany."

"'Maybe Germany' *and* you don't have the date *and* you aren't certain of the correct spelling of her name? You don't expect us to look through every application that has ever been archived, do you, Mr. O'Doyle?"

"Start in '46, Hanson."

"Honestly, Mr. O'Doyle, finding this application is going to be harder than finding a needle in a haystack. Are you sure she applied in Germany?"

"Just keep an eye out for the names while you sort the applications."

"Geez, Mr. O'Doyle, you don't give me anything to go on and you expect miracles. Washington wants every immigration application since '45 'fiched by the end of this year. I certainly don't have time for this nonsense."

"Listen to me good, Hanson. You *will* find the Goddamn immigration application, and if you don't find it, I'll go so far over your head you won't be able to see the bottom of my shoes. Is that clear, Hanson?"

O'Doyle sounded like a drill sergeant and took Hanson back to boot camp at Fort Grant in Rockford, Illinois, in April 1945. He snapped to attention and saluted. "What was the name, sir?"

 C3C3C3C3C3C3C3

A month later, O'Doyle was going through what seemed to be a mountain of mail on his desk. Louise had sliced open the envelopes and paper clipped the contents to the outside. When he saw the handwritten note clipped to an application that was obviously printed from microfiche, he yelled, "Jackpot!"

O'Doyle sprinted past Louise with a light brown interoffice envelope in his hands, down the stairs to the second floor, and stopped at the office with "George G. Linden, Director, US Immigration and Naturalization Service, Investigation Division, Chicago Office" painted on the frosted glass door. He took a minute to catch his breath and opened the door more forcefully than he intended. Miss Copley, Linden's latest secretary, was startled and dropped her nail file. She wore her long, blonde hair in big curls around her shoulders, and her red lipstick matched her nails, but the plunging neckline on her dark blue dress did not show anything to write home about.

"Is the director in?"

"I'll ask him." She reached to the intercom and flipped up the first switch. "Mr. Director, are you in?" He did not answer. She flipped the second switch and asked again.

"It might be faster if you just go look."

The secretary looked annoyed but took the suggestion. She opened the white painted door to her boss's office and immediately shielded her eyes from the glare of the late afternoon sun that streamed through the window. The walls were bare save for a cheap painting of a path through a bright forest. "Are you in, Mr. Linden? A man's here to see you."

He brought a fist onto the painted wood top of his government-issued metal desk. "Miss Copley, how many times have I told you . . . ? Isn't it obvious . . . ? Who is it?"

"He didn't say."

"You should have . . . oh, send him in."

O'Doyle closed the door and eased into a chair. "Oh boy, Chief, this new one's a doozy. Where did you get her?"

"Sheila got married and the typing pool sent this one. I can't find the idiot who hired her."

"Hah! Why don't you fire her? She can't be doing you any good."

"I can't for another few weeks. The wife said this girl won't last two months, and I have to prove her wrong if it's the last thing I do. But there's no use griping. What's going on, Hugh?"

"Chief, I have a hot one. A while back, I met with a Jewish couple, Mr. and Mrs. Berzon. Polish, I think. The wife said she saw a Nazi."

"A Nazi?" Linden leaned back. "Nobody cares about Nazis anymore."

"I know, but this one is different."

"They are all 'different.' Hugh, we have bigger things to worry about now. Hoover is still on the secretary's back about the Communists. Ever since Cuba it's—"

"Were you in Europe, Chief?"

Linden pointed to his thick, black-rimmed glasses. "4-F."

"You were lucky. I fought the Japs, but we both know about the Nazis, right, Chief? This one is special. This one was a *woman* guard at Auschwitz."

"A *woman*? Now, *that's* different. Let me see what you've got."

O'Doyle passed him the envelope, and Linden read the fuzzy photostat of the immigration application. "It says here she was a factory worker in Nuremberg. But you wouldn't expect her to list her occupation as 'Nazi,' do you?"

"I have a hunch this is the real deal."

"Hugh, your hunches don't always pan out. What makes you so sure about this one?"

"I can't really explain it. When I told Mrs. Berzon I couldn't help her, she didn't say anything, but I could see her knuckles turn white. There wasn't anything else about her that changed, but her hands gave her away. It made me feel like I would be letting every one of the victims down if I didn't try. Let me put someone on it."

Linden grinned. "I didn't know you were a Jew."

"Chief, I'm not, but I just have this feeling."

"Have it your way, Hugh. What's the plan for this caper?"

"I'd like to put someone on Roth for a few weeks. If there's nothing, I'll drop it."

"We're too short-staffed to go on a wild-goose chase."

"If we dig deep enough, there's gotta be something."

"You're going to have to do the investigation yourself, on your own time. And bring me results in thirty days, or this matter is closed. Capiche?" Linden flipped the switch labeled "Outer Office" on his intercom. . "Miss Copley, come in here."

No reply.

"Miss Copley, I said come in here."

Nothing.

O'Doyle bit his tongue as Linden stormed out of his office.

"Miss Copley, I summoned you on the intercom."

"I knew you'd come out."

Linden squeezed his eyes shut and balled his fists. *Damn it to hell!* He thought. *God knows, that woman has been right for thirty-years.*

He leaned over and said, just above a whisper, "Miss Copley, clean out your desk. You're fired."

Chapter 5. No Comparison

O'Doyle watched his sister, Tina, while she prepared steaks and corn on the cob for the barbecue. He had her by ten years and had become protective after their parents had died in a train accident in 1953. He'd discouraged Tina when she'd fallen in love with a guy from his high school class, but she'd dug in her heels. She was still happy with the guy and did not let her big brother forget that he'd been wrong. That was what O'Doyle loved most about Tina: she could really dish it out.

"Sis, a lady came into the office a couple of months ago. Mrs. Berzon, that's the lady's name, was at Auschwitz—you know, that Nazi concentration camp. She said she saw a woman who was a guard there. You shoulda seen her face when I told her there wasn't anything I could do." O'Doyle studied his cuticles. "I still feel terrible about that."

"Hugh, it's not your fault if you can't help, um, Mrs. Berzon. That is her name, right?"

"Yeah, but something is just not right about some Nazi living here."

Tina opened the refrigerator door. "You want a beer?"

"Thanks." He pulled the metal tab off the can and took a sip.

"You really aren't yourself! I don't think I've ever seen my big brother take such a dainty sip."

"Funny, sis. Anyway, I just couldn't get Mrs. Berzon out of my mind. Finally, it came to me. If that Nazi got some clerk to let her into the US, she must've lied on her immigration application."

Tina dropped three raw T-bone steaks onto a serving platter. "Makes sense to me, but I thought you said that these days it's the Communists taking up everybody's time."

"But, because this Nazi is a woman, the director gave me the go ahead and, here's the best part, I dug up some stuff that will help prove my case. My problem now is that I only have thirty days to figure out how I can get a judge to let me bring her in for interrogation." He picked up a mushroom and rolled it between his fingers. "Wally was with the 101st—he was at one of the camps."

Tina stopped shaking garlic powder onto the meat. "He never talks about it."

"He'll talk to me."

"Don't even ask."

"But, Sis, this is a matter of . . . well, maybe not life and death, but I can't just let that piece-of-work go on with her cushy life."

She opened a cupboard door and searched for a bottle of Worcestershire sauce. "Wally has terrible dreams. He thrashes around and yells, 'Stack the bodies over there, Kraut, before I make you one myself.' Sometimes he cries."

"That's exactly why I gotta talk to him. Besides, I saw things the Japs did that'd curl your hair."

Tina slammed the cupboard door. "Hugh, don't bother him."

"I've got to, Sis, I don't have anywhere else to go."

She leaned against the counter. Her stubborn big brother would not give up until he got his way. "If he doesn't want to talk, for God's sake, take 'no' for an answer."

"Scout's honor."

She raised an eyebrow. "You weren't a scout."

O'Doyle kissed Tina on the cheek and sauntered to the garage. He tried to act casual, but not too casual, when he saw his brother-in-law. "Hi, Wal, watcha doin'?"

"Just winding a fly. I'm taking the boy to Lake Geneva in the morning for a little bass fishing. He's still looking for the big one. You're welcome to come."

"No, thanks." O'Doyle sat on the hood of Wally's Lincoln.

Wally sensed his brother-in-law wanted something. "You have to be more careful with your money, Hugh. How much do you need this time?"

"Nothing. I have to talk to you about somethin' else."

"Shoot."

"A Polish couple came into the office a while back. The lady said she saw someone she recognized as a guard from one of the Nazi concentration camps."

"What about it?"

"It turns out the lady was right. I want to go after the Kraut, but I need to know more about the camps first."

"What's that got to do with me?"

"You were with the 101st, right?"

"Yeah."

"And you liberated one of the camps, right?"

"Stop right there, Hugh."

"You gotta help me."

"I guess the Japs took your hearing."

"C'mon, Wal."

Wally placed his son's fly into its proper compartment on the top tray of his tackle box. "You can't imagine how bad it was."

"I was at Iwo."

"Iwo was nothing compared to Dachau." He closed the metal lid on the red box and hoisted himself onto the wooden workbench. "All right, I'll talk about it, but don't ever, and I mean ever, ask me again."

O'Doyle scooted farther back on the hood of the car.

"We were closing in on Munich, and about ten miles out, we found a train with a bunch of cattle cars, sitting on the tracks. As we approached it, there was this smell—like rotting meat mixed with shit." Wally's words were steady. "When we got closer, we could see the bodies. There they were, with their eyes and mouths open, some of the heads were hanging out, almost touching the ground. And they were so skinny. They must have been so hungry, Hugh, that and—and I've never told anyone this—a couple of bodies were torn open. We didn't know what the hell was goin' on.

"We heard machine gun fire and found those Kraut bastards, standing around with machine guns, and about ten or so skinny guys, in the same striped uniforms as the bodies in the train, lined up against a wall. It wasn't more than a minute before the Krauts up and shot the prisoners. They just killed those poor guys, like you'd shoot rabbits or something. None of us moved until one of the Krauts started to line up more prisoners. One of our guys shot into the air. That got the Krauts' attention. Right away they dropped their weapons.

"Two of our guys lined up, I don't know, three or four Krauts, against the same wall and mowed 'em down. I heard they really caught some flak for that, but they did the exact right thing. I just wish I'd been the one to think of it."

"Wally, I had no—"

"Just listen, Hugh. Prisoners, and there were thousands of them, broke out of the barracks. They were all wearing the same uniforms and were as skinny as the guys in the train cars. They hugged and kissed every one of us. Nobody knew what they were saying, but we sure knew they were happy.

"We gave 'em all the food we had. They hadn't had food for so long that their bodies couldn't take it. We didn't mean to, but we killed some of 'em.

The docs told us to stop, and those poor guys just about rioted. You know, I was on Omaha and at Bastogne, and I was crying like a baby. And believe me, I wasn't the only one." He blew his nose into a white handkerchief. "You're wrong, Hugh. Compared to the Krauts, the Japs were nothing."

Chapter 6. Caught

Because Helga had been naturalized in 1957, O'Doyle needed airtight evidence before an immigration judge would agree to a deportation hearing. He read up on concentration camps but did not find much about women guards. He rummaged around the department's storage room and searched through dusty boxes filled with documents that had not been touched since the 1940s, until he found one with a handwritten sticker on the front: "Ravensbrück concentration camp—Women Prisoners Only—Trained Women Guards." He lit a cigarette then opened the file. "Elke Vogt interrogation 2/28/46. German transcript with English translation" was typed and perfectly centered on the title page.

Vogt's interrogation transcript showed she admitted to training women at Ravensbrück to be guards. She'd given details about how she'd taught the women to discipline prisoners, use pistols, truncheons, and whips. She'd bragged about her most successful trainees, then insisted she was just following orders.

O'Doyle read the transcript until he stumbled on Vogt's admiration for Helga Küster's natural abilities. *Jesus Christ, this is pure gold.*

ଔଔଔଔଔଔ

Helga dunked the mop head into a bucket of warm water when she heard heavy knocking. As she walked to the front door, she noticed a black car parked at the curb with "US Immigration and Naturalization Service" painted in white on the passenger door. She forgot her usual well-mannered niceties. "What do you want?"

"Mrs. Helga Roth?"

"Who are you?"

"My name is Hugh O'Doyle. I'm with the US Immigration and Naturalization Service. May I come in?"

"What do you want?"

"It would be best if we spoke inside. May I come in?"

"I am busy. Come back another time."

"I have a few questions, Mrs. Roth."

"I said—"

"This is too important to wait."

She opened the storm door, and he brushed past her.

"Let us sit down, Mr. O'Doyle."

He got comfortable in a dark brown leather chair and pulled a small notebook and ballpoint pen from his jacket. Helga took her place on the sofa and watched him leaf through the notebook to the first blank page and open the pen with his teeth.

"Are you Helga Roth, maiden name 'Küster'?"

"Yes."

"When did you arrive in the US, Mrs. Roth?"

"What is this about?"

"Please, just answer my questions."

"I arrived in the United States in 1947."

He jotted brief notes. "Your ship departed from Hamburg, Germany, and landed in Boston, Massachusetts. Is that correct?"

Helga's heart quickened. "Mr. O'Doyle, I insist you tell me what this is about."

"Did you have family in the US?" He noticed her breath was getting shallow.

"No, we did not require sponsorship for immigration."

"Before the war, what were your political affiliations?"

She paused longer than she should have. "I have no political affiliations."

O'Doyle looked around the front room. There was nothing to indicate Helga had an opinion about anything. Everything was in its place, but the room looked too sterile.

"Mrs. Roth, I asked about your political affiliations *before* the war."

"I am sorry, Mr. O'Doyle. As English is not my first language, I often become confused."

Bullshit, he thought. *You know exactly what I said.* "The question was straightforward, Mrs. Roth. What were your political affiliations before the war?"

"I was no Nazi, if that is your question."

"Of course not, none of you were." Right away he regretted saying that. "What was your husband's profession during the war?"

She wanted to defend her homeland, but simply answered the question. "He worked in a factory."

"He was not in the Gestapo or SS?"

"No, Mr. O'Doyle. My husband, Markus, has had a weak heart since childhood and was not suited to be a soldier."

"Have you found fellow Germans, people in your same situation, who you and your husband have become acquainted with since you've been in the States?"

Helga's patience grew thin. "I demand to know why you are asking these questions, Mr. O'Doyle. One cannot simply enter someone else's home and ask such personal questions."

"We are almost done."

"You understand that one cannot survive without friends, do you not?"

"Did you know them in Germany?"

"We met them when we moved into this house."

"What were your new friends' political affiliations back in Germany?"

"We do not speak of politics, Mr. O'Doyle."

"That's hard to believe. Do you and your friends get together often?"

"Yes, Markus and I host our friends every Thursday night to talk about the things we miss from our homeland."

"What are those things, Mrs. Roth?"

"We miss the same things anyone would—our homes, our families, the food, and the beauty of our country."

"You were quite young when Hitler took power, weren't you?"

"That is quite enough. It is time for you to leave."

"Just answer the question."

"I am a citizen of the United States of America and I will not allow you to interrogate me as if I were a criminal."

He noticed her increasing irritation. "You were quite young when Hitler became the Führer, weren't you?"

"I was thirteen years old in 1933."

"Thirteen is a very impressionable age, isn't it?"

Her face flushed in anger. "You must leave now, Mr. O'Doyle. Come back when my husband is home."

"You and your friends miss the Führer, don't you?"

"I have nothing more to say. Please leave."

"Every Thursday night, you and your friends pretend that you never lost the war and—"

The veins in her neck bulged. "You are here because of that Jew. We should have killed them all!"

O'Doyle re-capped his pen and slid it into the notebook's spiral. "Mrs. Roth, come with me."

CRCRCRCRCRCR

O'Doyle chain-smoked and watched pigeons on his windowsill. Questions about how or why Helga would do those horrible things to another human being swirled inside his head. In a strange way, he understood how a soldier could commit horrible acts against another soldier—that is what they are trained to do. Louise entered his office, interrupting his thoughts.

"Mr. O'Doyle, Helga Roth is on seven."

"Let's get this show on the road."

They took the elevator up to the seventh floor. O'Doyle followed Louise into a small foyer behind a door marked "US Immigration and Naturalization Service—Interrogations."

"Hello, Mr. O'Doyle," the pretty receptionist said. "Mrs. Roth is waiting in fourteen."

"Thanks, doll. Louise, go set up; I'll be there in a minute."

Louise went down the long hallway and tapped as she opened the door marked "Room 14."

The windowless room with harsh fluorescent lighting made Helga appear gray and drab. Louise did not speak as she arranged a stack of file folders, two legal pads, four Paper Mate clip pens, a pack of Lucky Strikes, and a square, glass ashtray on the black wood table. The long-time secretary knew the exact position for each item: paper and pens on O'Doyle's left, files on the right, and smokes directly in front of him. Louise left without looking at Helga.

"Everything is all ready, Mr. O'Doyle."

"Thanks, Louise. Wish me luck."

"Go get 'em."

O'Doyle hesitated a second, then opened the door. He draped his suit jacket over the back of his chair, took his seat, picked up the cigarettes, and tamped the pack on the table; he did not want tobacco sticking to his tongue. After he stripped off the plastic band and opened the pack, he gestured across the table. "Smoke?"

"No, thank you."

"Have it your way." He put a cigarette between his lips and deftly flipped a Zippo that had an aircraft carrier engraved on the front. A few snaps of the metal wheel against the flint and a spark connected with lighter fluid. He cupped his free hand around the flame—an old habit from the war, when the lighter was no match for the winds that whipped across the deck of the USS *Saratoga*. The first long drag filled his lungs, and he held the smoke in for a second or two before he blew smoke rings to the ceiling. "Mrs. Roth, you were a kid when Hitler came to power, correct?"

"Yes."

"What did you think of Hitler?" He stayed friendly to keep her at ease.

"I had no thoughts of Hitler. I was busy with school and my friends."

"What did your father think of Hitler?"

"My father did not discuss politics with his children." *Why do Americans think parents should discuss everything with their children?* Helga thought.

"Your father never shared an opinion with your family about the state of the country? Not even once?"

"No, Mr. O'Doyle. Unlike you Americans, German parents do not include children in discussions about politics."

Smoke from O'Doyle's cigarette collected on the ceiling, adding to the stuffiness of the small room. He loosened his tie and unbuttoned the top button of his white dress shirt. She looked at him with a mixture of contempt and superiority. She was not bothered by a bit of discomfort.

"On your immigration application, you said you were a member of the BDM. What was the BDM?"

"The Bund Deutscher Mädel. It was a social club."

"What does it mean in English?"

"In English, it loosely means League of German Girls. It was like the Hitler Youth, but for girls."

He pulled another drag from his cigarette. "What did you do in this 'social club'?"

"We participated in athletic events, hiked and swam and learned to become good German wives and mothers."

"So, even though the Hitler Youth was very political, the BDM was not?" He exhaled the smoke toward her.

"You Americans think everything in Germany was 'Hitler, Hitler, Hitler.' That is not how it was, Mr. O'Doyle. We did not march around like little plastic soldiers." She fanned the smoke away from her face. "I must say you are very rude."

He flicked the cigarette ash into the ashtray with his thumb. "How many Jewish girls were in your BDM group, Mrs. Roth?"

"Jewish girls? Well, there would not have been any, Mr. O'Doyle. Jews were not welcome in the BDM. Jews had their own groups."

"Are Jews a problem for you, Mrs. Roth?"

Helga took stock of the room, noticing the walls, door, and floor. The floor had dozens of cigarette burns, and the walls, except for the light switch, were covered in nicotine. On the back of the door there was a coat hook, hanging by one screw. "I do not understand the question."

He leaned back until the chair teetered on two legs. "What I mean is, how do you feel about the Jews?"

"I have no feeling for the Jews."

"So, it did not bother you that Jews were not allowed to join the BDM."

"Why would it? That is just the way it was."

"Were you happy Jews could not join, Mrs. Roth?"

Helga's jaw stiffened. "Mr. O'Doyle, it was of no concern to me."

"In 1940, you went to Ravensbrück concentration camp to start a job." He coaxed another cigarette out of the pack. "Is that correct?"

"That is incorrect." She pushed a stray strand of hair behind her ear.

"You did *not* go to Ravensbrück?"

"Yes, that is correct."

"Are you sure you were never at Ravensbrück? Maybe you forgot."

"I could not *forget*, because I was never there."

"You did not receive guard training at Ravensbrück?"

"I could not have, as I never went to this 'Ravensbrück.'"

"Let's stop this cat and mouse game, Mrs. Roth. I have evidence that you went through guard training at Ravensbrück."

Helga felt all the air get sucked out of the room. O'Doyle had much more information that she thought possible. If he had proof of her time at Ravensbrück, he might have learned about Auschwitz. "Mr. O'Doyle, I do not lie when I say that I did not leave Nuremberg during the war."

"I have evidence that says otherwise."

"Your so-called evidence is untrue."

Although he had memorized her application he glanced at it, just for show. "Mrs. Roth, I don't see any mention of the BDM or Ravensbrück on your immigration application."

"I tell you again, I was a war worker at a defense plant. I hated the Nazis, just like everyone."

"What was your job at the plant, Mrs. Roth?"

"I assembled transmissions for panzers. I believe the English word is 'tanks.'"

"That is interesting, considering that Hitler preferred to use slave labor."

"I contributed to the war effort, like any good German."

"Who was your employer?"

"Mr. O'Doyle, I do not remember."

"You don't remember the name of your employer during the war?"

"English is not my first language. I am getting confused."

"I think your English is pretty good, Mrs. Roth, but I don't want you to be confused. Take a moment to think. What was the name of your employer during the war?"

"*Bayerische*—no, you would say 'Bavarian Motor Works.'"

"Now we are getting somewhere. What did you do for BMW?"

"I have already told you—I assembled transmissions for tanks. I was essential to the war effort."

"Ya know what's funny, Mrs. Roth? BMW didn't build their factory in Nuremburg until after the war."

"You cannot know every factory in Nuremberg. There were so many American bombings that we could not distinguish one building from the next."

"On your application, you said you assembled tank transmissions at this ghost factory, right?"

"Mr. O'Doyle, I have stated that I assembled tank transmissions for BMW."

He slid her application across the table. "Take a closer look. Read the answer on line twenty-five, 'Occupation during the war.'"

She ran her finger down the page. For a moment, she was not sure she remembered what she wrote on the form almost two decades before. "I see that I wrote 'housewife' as my occupation during the war. You must forgive me, Mr. O'Doyle, if when I completed this form, I did not fully understand the question. My answer to that question was the best I could give, as I did not understand very much English at the time."

"You chose to write 'housewife' instead of 'factory worker'? That is a big difference."

"No, Mr. O'Doyle. It was not the occupation, but the time. I did not understand what 'during the war' meant. I was a housewife when my husband and I came to the United States."

"Let's say I believe that, which I don't, that still doesn't answer what you did during the war. You won't convince me BMW had a factory in Nuremberg at that time. Plus, BMW made aircraft engines, not tank transmissions. Know what? I don't think you were in Nuremberg during the war at all."

Helga's words were deliberate. "I assembled tank transmissions at the BMW plant."

"Let's get back to your application. Read your answer to question number twenty-six, 'List all Political Party affiliations.'"

"Again, Mr. O'Doyle"—she did not reference the application—"my answer was truthful in that I had no political affiliations."

"I find it very difficult to believe that you understood the phrase 'during the war' as it appeared on line twenty-six, but not on line twenty-five."

"I was not political then, nor am I now."

Now I've got her. "Mrs. Roth are you aware that you have been under surveillance for quite some time?"

"I beg your pardon?"

"You host a group of Nazis in your home every week."

"My friends are not Nazis. We are simply Germans who are homesick for the old days."

"You want me to believe that eight Germans who lived in the Third Reich get together every week and not one of them was ever a Nazi?"

She cleared her throat. "I have answered enough questions. I would like to return home."

"Not yet. I want to know more about your weekly meetings. You say you don't discuss politics, so what do you and your friends talk about?"

Helga's accent thickened. "Ve talk about zee old days, zing German zongs and eat German food. Zeese parties vould be qvite dull for non-Germans."

"Mrs. Roth, perhaps it is time for you to come clean."

"Vhat is dis 'come clean'?"

"It means 'tell the Goddamn truth.'"

She regained her composure. "Perhaps it is *you* who is lying, Mr. O'Doyle."

"Nice try, Mrs. Roth. I am taking you into custody until I can arrange a deportation hearing. Someone will be here in a minute to take you to your new home. I have a call to make."

ೞೞೞೞೞೞ

Rose was copying a recipe from a magazine when the telephone rang. "Hello."

"Mrs. Berzon? Hugh O'Doyle from the INS. I have good news. We have Helga Roth in custody. Next, we have to get a judge to order a deportation hearing, but that should be easy. The thing is, we are going to need you at the hearing. I know that it won't be easy, but it is important that you are at the hearing, okay? I'll be in touch to let you know when the hearing is and the attorney's name who will help you get prepared. Talk to you soon."

Rose trembled, and tears fell down her face until she found the strength to hang up the telephone receiver.

೫೫೫೫೫೫೫

Two days after O'Doyle called Rose with the news, the INS attorney, John Christensen, called to make an appointment. She agreed to meet with him the next day, then went to bed, where she did not move or talk. Samuel sent the boys to stay at a neighbor's house until the hearing was over. It was too much to ask them to witness what was to come.

Christensen arrived at Rose's home the next morning at ten o'clock and rang the doorbell. Samuel welcomed him and offered him coffee.

"Thank you, but no thank you, Mr. Berzon. I've had enough coffee for today. Will Mrs. Berzon be joining us soon?"

"I want to talk to you before Rose comes down. This is very hard for her, Mr. Christensen. She has not spoken a word since you called yesterday, and I am afraid she will not be able to go through with this."

"This must be almost unbearable for her, and I suppose for you, too. But, I'm afraid this is the only way to make sure Mrs. Roth is deported. She said ugly things during her interrogation, but that is not enough for deportation. We were lucky the judge was willing to have a hearing at all."

"Just be aware, Mr. Christensen, that I only ask you to remember that my wife is very fragile. Please make yourself comfortable, and I will get Rose."

Christensen had not brought a briefcase. He wanted to meet Rose and just get to know her to see if she would be credible on the stand. He did not doubt her honesty or sincerity, but this was a precedent-setting case, and he wanted to do everything right.

He heard who he guessed was Rose and Samuel in low conversation but could not distinguish the words until they were almost in the room, when he realized they were speaking Yiddish. He saw the couple stop short and Samuel whispered into Rose's ear. She smiled and nodded.

"Mr. Christensen, I am Rose Berzon. Welcome to our home."

She was short, less than five feet tall, and slim with wrinkles on her face that made her look much older than she was. Christensen understood the wrinkles came from trauma, not the passage of time. "Mrs. Berzon, it is my pleasure. Thank you for meeting with me so quickly. I will get to the point. The INS has obtained permission to have a hearing to decide if Mrs. Roth should be allowed to stay in the country or be deported back to Germany. This is highly unusual, because there is no evidence of any wrongdoing since her arrival. Regardless of the outcome, this could set the precedent for future deportations."

Rose held his eyes and did not blink until she finished speaking. "Please, allow me to stop you there, Mr. Christensen. I understand the situation and how important this case is, but I am not interested in setting a precedent or being important. She should not be allowed to stay in this country and that is why I will testify."

Christensen was at a loss for words. He had not expected the amount of strength she projected in that one statement. That is when he noticed the way she crossed her legs at the ankles while she sat across from him and how her hands were folded. She was so cultured and dainty and strong all at the same time. She was perfect for the stand. "That is exactly what I hoped you would say. The hearing has not been scheduled yet, but I am told it will be in about eight weeks. That gives us enough time to prepare."

"What exactly do you need me to do?"

"I need you to tell your story—how you met Mrs. Roth at Auschwitz, and what she did there."

Samuel said, "That is too much. Rose, can you do that?"

"Yes, Samuel, I will try. Please continue, Mr. Christensen."

"That's really all I need from you. I have the evidence from the INS, which is pretty damning. It's just going to be important that the judge sees Mrs. Roth's victim as a human being, not words on a page."

Rose nodded.

"I have to tell you one more thing, Mrs. Berzon. Mrs. Roth's attorney will have the opportunity to ask you questions, and his questions might be very upsetting."

"What kind of questions?"

"He might twist your words or try to get you to say you are exaggerating—"

"Mr. Christensen, there is no need to exaggerate anything at Auschwitz."

"I understand, but that is how these hearings work and I am going to do my best to prepare you for anything the defense says. You have to trust me."

ରେଉରେଉରେଉରେଉ

Helga waited in the reception room next to the INS holding cells, where she had been held for seven weeks. No one had visited her because everyone she knew was afraid of being interrogated. She passed the time by fantasizing about what she would do when she was freed. She would hunt down the Jew who tried to get her deported, and that Jew would pay dearly. Because Markus had initiated divorce proceedings and left Helga destitute, the INS appointed her a public defender. She stood up when a middle-aged man entered and offered his hand.

"Hello, Mrs. Roth. I'm Ed Huber, the defense attorney appointed to represent you at your deportation hearing."

"It is a pleasure to meet you, Mr. Huber. Shall we get to work?"

He set a yellow legal pad on the table, then screwed off the top of his Montblanc pen. "Tell me about how you know Mrs. Rose Berzon."

"What happens during the hearing, Mr. Huber?"

"Here's how this goes. You will stay in INS custody. Just like a jury trial, the prosecution presents their case. After that, it's our turn. Then the judge will take a few days to decide if you stay in the US."

"I should not be kept in a cage like an animal."

"May I call you Helga? Helga, I'm sorry about this inconvenience. You'll be home in no time."

"When is this hearing?"

"Two weeks from today. I expect it'll last maybe three days, and it might take another three or four days for the judge to make his decision. This should all be over by the end of the month—middle of next, at the latest."

"That is a long time from now, Mr. Huber."

"I understand, but for the next two weeks, you and I will spend a lot of time together. We will talk about the INS evidence, what questions they might ask, and rehearse your answers."

"Mr. Huber, I do not want to be questioned."

"It is important that you tell your story in your own words. Don't worry; it is my job to make sure you are ready. I have to tell you, Helga, there might be a hitch in your case. Since the Eichmann trial in Israel a couple of years back, the US government has been in talks with West Germany about prosecuting ex-Nazis."

"What has that got to do with me?"

"Frankly, there is some pretty damning evidence. The INS found an interrogation transcript of a woman named Elke Vogt. She claimed she was at Ravensbrück concentration camp and trained the new guards. She also said you were her best student and she promoted you to instructor. And then there's the transcript of your conversation with the INS. It looks like you had some kind of an outburst about the Jews."

Helga was stone-faced. "Mr. Huber, why is the world not grateful for our efforts to exterminate the Jews?"

"Mrs. Roth, don't say anything like that during the hearing."

Chapter 7. Bear with Me

After thirty-six years on the bench, Edwin Bodden was known throughout the INS as tough but fair in deportation hearings. "Gentlemen, Mrs. Roth is a naturalized citizen of the United States of America, and I take an attempt to deport a naturalized citizen very seriously. I do not tolerate shenanigans during hearings. Mr. Christensen, you may begin."

"Your Honor, in the midst of the chaos after World War Two, Mrs. Roth submitted an application to immigrate to the United States of America, omitting evidence of her Nazi past. She was granted access to the United States and eventually became a naturalized citizen. It was not until Mrs. Rose Berzon, a survivor of the Nazi concentration camps, happened to see Mrs. Roth in an ordinary grocery store and bravely came forward that the Immigration and Naturalization Service discovered the heinous crimes Mrs. Roth hid with her lies.

"I agree with Your Honor. The decision to deport a naturalized citizen should not be taken lightly. Please bear with me while I tell you the story of Mrs. Helga Roth and Mrs. Rose Berzon, one German, one Polish, whose lives collided during man's darkest days."

PART II. TWO LIVES

1936

Chapter 8. Disbelief

A few residents in Kraków's Jewish Quarter had gathered at the Old Synagogue to compare letters from family and friends in Germany. "These stories are too fantastic to believe."

"What an imagination your brother—or cousin or friend—has. This is not the Middle Ages."

"Granted, there may have been some violence against Jews in Germany, so what is new?"

"This will pass, it always has."

Rose Goldberg, her husband, Jacob, and her parents, lived in a flat near the Vistula River. Shyke Silverstein, Rose's father, owned a bookstore on Szeroka Street and had gifted half of the business to his daughter and son-in-law on their wedding day. The bookstore sold rare volumes from Jewish and Polish writers. Jews and Gentiles were often seen browsing through sagging bookshelves and tall stacks of books, helping one another search for a treasured find.

In the summer of 1936, Yiddish radio stations in Kraków often interrupted the popular Jewish comedy skits and music with news about Polish athletes at Berlin's Summer Olympics. The Poles were no match for the Germans and Americans; nonetheless, it was fun to hear vivid descriptions of the events.

Rose's mother, Pesche, held up a flower-patterned dress. "Rose, put this on."

"Just a minute, Mama." Rose set aside the sock stretched over a wooden darning egg and stepped onto a black leather ottoman. She carefully pulled the dress over her head, so as not to prick herself with the straight pins holding the hem in place.

"The hem is perfect, but it seems a little tight at the waist. You can take it off now, Rose."

Jacob turned the page of his newspaper. "All I read anymore is Hitler this and Hitler that."

"None of that matters to us," Rose said.

Shyke turned up the volume on the radio. "Rose is right; there are much more interesting things in this world. I would like to hear about the Olympics."

"With all due respect, Hitler is causing a great deal of trouble for the Jews. He demands they leave Germany, then makes it impossible with exit fees so large that only the rich can pay. Where are they supposed to go? The United States will not even accept them."

"That is a shame, Jacob."

"Shyke, you must not be naïve."

"Why do we have to listen to bad news?" Pesche asked.

"I agree with Mama," Rose said, reaching for the radio. "We should listen to music."

"Wait, they are talking about Berlin." Shyke leaned in close.

> *The Track and Field events today saw the American Negro, Jesse Owens, set another world record. Owens bested Germany's Luz Long in the men's long jump with 8.06 meters to Long's 7.87 meters. Germany's führer, Adolf Hitler, did not witness his country's latest loss. He exited the Olympic Stadium when three American Negroes—Cornelius Johnson, Dave Albritton, and Delos Thurber—swept the men's high jump event earlier in the day. It is reported Hitler is infuriated by the German losses and has vowed not to return to the Stadium.*

"Hah! That will teach that *mamzer* about 'inferior races.'"

"Shyke, I think he is more of a . . . *kafin kup*."

"Mama, such language!"

"Hitler deserves the title, my darling. Now, let me finish this hem." Pesche laid the skirt on her lap and, by hand, sewed perfect, even stitches.

"Your mother is correct, Rose. Hitler is set on humiliating Germany's Jews."

"You talk as if he is standing on our doorstep." Rose lightly patted a silver coffee carafe on the wooden buffet behind the dinner table. Satisfied the coffee was still warm, she refilled Jacob's cup. "It is all just politics. Nothing will come of it."

Pesche closed the lid on her sewing kit. "We have had enough political talk for one evening. Let us discuss the grandchildren I am still waiting for."

"Rose and I want to live on our own before we start a family."

Shyke tried to stop his wife from being a meddling mother-in-law. "Do not mix in with the children, Pesche."

"I asked when they will give me grandchildren. Is that a crime?"

"Pesche, we want to be on our own before we start a family, and I have not saved enough money."

"Nonsense, Jacob. Shyke and I started our family the proper way—on our wedding night—and lived with my mama and papa until Rose was three years old. That was good enough for us. By the time you two are ready, I will be too old for grandchildren."

Rose touched her mother's arm. "Mama, we are simply being practical."

"Pesche, do you remember how your mama tried to mix in with us?" Shyke said.

"That was different. When we married, we did not need advice."

"Mama, you were only sixteen when you married Papa. I promise that Jacob and I will have children when we are ready."

With a Jewish mother's guilt-inducing wail, Pesche pounded her chest and beseeched God, "*Oy*, why do you not bless me with grandchildren? What have I done to deserve this?"

Rose rolled her eyes.

"They are in no hurry, Pesche. Our grandchildren will come in due time. And if that time is never, then so be it."

Jacob put his arm around his wife's thickening waist. "Shyke, Pesche. We did not want to give you the news yet, but—"

"My baby is expecting!" Pesche hugged Rose. "What took you so long?"

"Mama, we were married less than a year ago."

"Son"—Shyke shook Jacob's hand—"the old saying is true: man plans, God laughs."

1937

Chapter 9. Family Disappearance

Yossel, a freelance writer, had not sold a story in two years, because no German magazine or newspaper would buy from Jews. Sieglinde's job in a flag factory did not pay enough to support them, and they often dined with Fredderecke, Cäcilia, and Helga.

"Mother, will Sieglinde and that Jew be here for dinner again?"

"Sieglinde and Yossel are joining us."

Helga poured a glass of juice. "Father should not support that Jew."

Cäcilia skinned a potato with punishing strokes. "Your sister loves Yossel, and because Sieglinde loves him, we love him."

"But, Mother," Helga protested, "they are here almost every night. Must they come on Sundays, too?"

"Your sister and her husband are family." She sliced her finger and watched the blood disappear down the drain. "Go wash your hands."

Helga ran to her father. "Father, you must stop Mother. She cannot continue to feed that Jew."

"Your mother will do as she sees fit."

"I insist you and Mother stop wasting food on a Jew."

Fredderecke jumped out of his chair and slapped his daughter. "You do nothing but spout garbage."

"That filthy Jew should have left Germany long ago."

Cäcilia burst into the room. "Fredderecke, what happened?"

"I order you to stop this nonsense, or I swear, Helga, I will—"

"Fredderecke, do not say anything you will regret." Cäcilia gently dabbed blood from Helga's lip. "Your father and I did not teach you to say those things. We must all be respectful of each other."

Sieglinde poked her head in from the front door. "Hello. Is anyone home? We smell something wonderful."

Fredderecke warned Helga to behave, then greeted Sieglinde and Yossel. "It is so good to see you both." He shook his son-in-law's hand. "How is the writing business, Yossel?"

"I have heard nothing, Fredderecke."

Cäcilia stroked his arm. "How discouraging. You could submit stories using Sieglinde's name."

"Mother, my last name is Veilchenfeld, remember?" She hugged her mother's shoulders.

Cäcilia squeezed back. "You could use 'Küster.' That is a fine German name."

Sieglinde's eyes lit up. "Yossel, what do you think?"

"That might work." Yossel tugged his Vandyke. "Are you sure you want your name on something written by a Jew?"

She threw her arms around him. "I would be proud."

Helga listened to the chatter with a cold, damp cloth pressed against her swollen lip.

"What happened to your lip?" Yossel asked.

"Father—"

"Sieglinde," Fredderecke interrupted, "I do not know why the Führer is still so damned set on blaming the Jews for everything."

Cäcilia shooed the family to the dining table and served roast chicken, boiled carrots, and sauerkraut.

"Do not get upset, Fredderecke," Cäcilia said, as she placed her hand over his. "Remember what Dr. Veilchenfeld said."

"You saw my father? Is he doing well?"

"He is doing as well as he can under the circumstances," Fredderecke said "It is such a pity his talents are wasting away."

Sieglinde's eyes welled up. "Father, that was a very dangerous thing to do."

"I was not feeling well," Fredderecke said as he leaned back. "And I wanted to see the best man I knew. It is as simple as that."

"And because your father is a baby, it helps that Yossel's father is a pediatrician."

"Yes, my dear, that is exactly why I sought out the good doctor."

Helga slammed her fist on the table. "Father, you could be arrested!"

Sieglinde threw her napkin to her plate. "Hitler cannot make everyone a Nazi."

"Here, here," Fredderecke said as he forked a chicken leg.

"Fredderecke, you have had enough. Helga, you and your sister clean up, while your father, Yossel, and I talk."

"I cannot keep this secret any longer. Yossel and I are having a baby."

Cäcilia threw her arms around her oldest daughter. "A baby! What a grand surprise."

"Well, Yossel," Fredderecke said, "you have a family now. Are you ready for this?"

Yossel raked an unsteady hand through his hair. "It appears that I must be, Fredderecke."

"Son"—he chuckled—"there is nothing you can do now."

Helga watched the scene with utter disgust.

When Cäcilia regained her composure, she said, "Helga, please clean up the table. The four of us have quite a bit to talk about."

"I will help you," Sieglinde volunteered.

"Stay here. You should not work in your condition."

"Mother, I am not sick. I am having a baby!"

Helga filled the kitchen sink with warm, soapy water and added several glasses. She sloppily ran a sponge over and into each glass, then dipped it into warm, clear water. Sieglinde inspected each glass and dried only those without spots.

"Mother said you were at that stupid Party rally. How can you stand to be with those blowhards?" Sieglinde held a glass up to the light. "Those lunatics are horrible. Each one is worse than the last."

"German women must always do their duty for the Führer."

"Hitler gets positively apoplectic during his speeches."

Helga narrowed her eyes and clenched her teeth. "Do not ever say that."

Sieglinde was not fazed by Helga's threat. "I will say what I want."

"Everyone gossips about you and your Jew. It is embarrassing."

"I simply will not live my life for the small-minded."

Without warning, Helga punched her sister in the stomach and stood over her as she fell to the floor from the force of the blow. "Jew-loving whore."

Fredderecke charged in to the kitchen "What happened? What is going on?"

Yossel fell beside his wife and cradled her head in his lap as a pool of blood soaked through her dress and stained the floor. "Sieglinde, what happened?"

Sieglinde looked at Helga. "You killed my baby. You will burn in hell."

Self-satisfied, Helga simply said, "We cannot have some half-Jew bastard in the family."

Cäcilia folded her hands and pleaded to the ceiling, "Dear God, why did you give me a second child?"

CRCRCRCRCRCR

The next morning, Helga woke late and left the house without breakfast. Cäcilia stayed in bed until her daughter was gone.

Helga squeezed into a tramcar for the short ride to the Palace of Justice. When she arrived, she went straight to the information desk and waited for the fresh-faced Gestapo agent to finish his obscene doodle of a naked woman with her back arched over a swastika. He looked up when Helga blocked his light. "What is your business?"

"I must report a criminal."

"Denouncement?"

"Yes."

"Top of the stairs, turn right, second door on the left."

More than fifty Nurembergers waited in line to denounce their friends and neighbors. For many, the lure of making easy money was enough for them to pay attention to even the smallest details of the rules and regulations the Nazis had instituted. Helga recognized the last person in line.

"Hello, Mr. Pfeffer."

"Helga! Such a lovely surprise." Conrad Pfeffer was sloppily fat and believed he hid his baldness by combing his greasy hair over the top of his head. "How are your parents and your sister?"

"They are all doing well, thank you. Mr. Pfeffer, have you been waiting long?"

"Approximately one hour. I suspect there are too few interviewers today. Every day last week lines were very short, and the wait was no more than five minutes."

Before Pfeffer made a living by denouncing his neighbors, he had worked for an automobile manufacturer as an accountant. The wages were adequate to remain in the middle class of German society, but he was determined to join the upper classes. He had accumulated his wealth so rapidly that rumors had spread of his ability to concoct infractions based on reward levels.

Helga laughed. "Hopefully we will not wait very much longer."

"Do you expect today will be profitable for you, my dear?"

"It depends. How much does a Jew bring these days?"

He opened a leather-bound accounting ledger, but the usual column headings, Explanation, Debit, and Credit were crossed out and replaced with Name, Description, and Estimated Reward. He had drawn a fourth column titled: Actual Reward. The subtotals for the reward columns had nearly worn through the page from Pfeffer's daily recalculations.

Helga peeked at the page. "Mr. Pfeffer, why do you have two amount columns?"

"I play a little game with myself. When I record an infraction, I estimate the reward, then record the actual. For example, look at my very first entry." He flipped to the first page. "'Wieck, Nadine. Entered Jew store. Estimated Amount: ten. Actual Amount: three.'" He winked. "I have become much more accurate with my estimates."

"How much do you get for a typical Jew?"

"My last Jew was"—he searched backward from the last used page—"Tuesday of last week. My estimate was somewhat off. I predicted the reward to be forty-five marks, but as luck would have it, the reward was increased to fifty."

"Fifty?"

"This line of work is very profitable, Helga. I highly recommend it."

Soon, a Gestapo officer waved Helga to his desk. "Heil Hitler. Please sit down, miss. Name?"

"Helga Küster."

"Complaint?"

"I wish to report a Jew."

He rolled a form into the typewriter. "Name and address of the Jew."

She provided Yossel's information.

"That is all I need." He reached for a small pad of forms marked "Voucher" and wrote "75" on the amount line. "Take this to the first-floor cashier."

∞∞∞∞∞∞∞

"Gestapo. Open up."

Yossel dropped the spool of a half-installed typewriter ribbon. In his panic, he forgot the window in the bedroom was locked. It was no use. The agents in long black leather coats broke through the door and violently handcuffed him. They confirmed his name, picked him up by the cuffs, and shoved him down the stairs. An unmarked car waited in the street with its rear door open. Yossel's head hit the roof of the car as they threw him onto the back seat. Silent bystanders watched the scene until the car sped away.

The busybody in the flat across the hall from Sieglinde's, Mrs. Proch, could not wait to spread the news and called her friend who lived on the building's top floor. "The Jew is finally gone. What? Why did you stay quiet? Next time tell me. Wait. I think I hear that woman. Goodbye."

Sieglinde had stopped to buy vegetables on her walk home from the flag factory. She worked ten hours a day, six days a week, hemming huge Nazi banners. After the tedium of the day, she looked forward to a quiet evening with her husband.

"Oh, Mrs. Veilchenfeld." Mrs. Proch feigned surprise as she met Sieglinde on the landing. "I did not hear you. You poor thing, I have bad news."

Sieglinde sighed. "Can this wait?"

"I am afraid not, dear. The Gestapo was here and took your husband. He is a Jew, correct? We cannot have Jews here."

Sieglinde dropped the groceries and ran to the street. She hailed a taxi and begged the driver to hurry. When the taxi stopped in front of the Palace of Justice, she threw the fare onto the front seat and bolted into the converted courthouse.

The same fresh-faced Gestapo agent who had directed Helga to the office to denounce Yossel, pointed Sieglinde to the office that oversaw the cells where he was being held. A tall man dressed in a dark suit balanced a telephone receiver between his head and his shoulder while he wrote on a small pad. "Yes, sir. I will tell him the moment he arrives. Heil Hitler."

Sieglinde was out of breath and could barely speak. "You must tell me where my husband is. His name is—"

"I cannot understand you, please slow down. Who are you looking for?"

"I am here for my husband."

"Madam, there is no need for rudeness. What is the name?"

"Yossel Veilchenfeld. V-E-I-L-C-H-E-N-F-E-L-D."

He ran his finger down the list of inmates. "It says here he is in protective custody for an undetermined period."

"What is 'protective custody'?"

"Jews must be held to ensure their safety."

"Sir, I will take full responsibility for my husband's safety. Please release him into my care."

"Forget about him. A nice German girl like you should not be with a Jew. Heil Hitler."

Biting her lip hard to keep the tears from falling, Sieglinde exited the office and ran into a telephone booth outside. "The Gestapo is holding Yossel in 'protective custody.' Mother, what can I do?"

"Calm down, Sieglinde. Where are you?"

"I am at Gestapo headquarters."

"Go to your flat. Your father will be there soon."

"This is a nightmare." Sieglinde felt the annoyed glare from the young Gestapo agent and, in a wordless condemnation of injustice, slammed the phone into its place.

ରେଜେଜେଜେ

Fredderecke reached the landing near Sieglinde's flat when Mrs. Proch appeared from thin air.

"Good evening, Mr. Küster. I am sorry to see you under such circumstances."

Her sickening sweet smile made him wish he were not a gentleman. "Good evening."

"I happened to be home and saw the whole thing. It was terrible how those men treated your poor Yossel. I have a chicken in the oven, and I am certain you would like to comfort your daughter. It is always a pleasure, Mr. Küster. I hope to see you again, under happier circumstances, of course."

Fredderecke had barely entered the flat when Sieglinde threw open her bedroom door and launched herself into her father's arms, crying until he felt her tears through his vest.

"There, there, Sieglinde, we must be brave. You will stay with your mother and I until Yossel is released."

They both knew he was lying. Jews were never released. Jews vanished.

ରେଜେଜେଜେ

"Mother, who was on the telephone?"

"The Gestapo arrested Yossel." Cäcilia wrung her hands. "Your father is bringing your sister home. You and Sieglinde will share your room."

Helga pushed her braids behind her and put on a coat.

"Where do you think you are going?"

"I have a BDM meeting."

"Not tonight," Cäcilia said. "You will stay here and wait for your sister."

"All of this because some damn Jew was arrested?"

The front door opened.

"They are here." Cäcilia cautioned. "You will not upset your sister further."

Sieglinde ran to her mother and sobbed. Helga was repulsed by the scene.

"Hug your sister," Fredderecke whispered as he nudged his youngest daughter.

She brushed him off.

"I said, go to your sister."

Helga snarled. "She should not be married to that Jew."

"You evil witch." Sieglinde pointed at her sister. "You turned him in!"

"No," Helga lied. "But I should have, you lousy Jew-lover."

1938

Chapter 10. *Kristallnacht*

O n November 9, 1938, violence against the Jews broke out in every corner of the Third Reich. It was said the rioting had broken out spontaneously in response to the assassination of a low-level German diplomat in Paris by a young Jewish man. In truth, German leaders had encouraged the youth to harass Jews and set synagogues on fire. That night became known as *Kristallnacht*, or "Night of Broken Glass," due to the sheer number of shop windows destroyed. Helga had heard the radio reports of the rioting against the Jews and changed into her BDM uniform.

Cäcilia was finishing cleaning the kitchen after dinner, and Fredderecke was reading the newspaper in his favorite chair. He thought he heard someone cough outside and peeked out the window.

"Cäcilia," Fredderecke called out, "wrap up the last of the *Zwiebelkuchen*. Conrad Pfeffer is coming."

"Be careful, Fredderecke. He wants more than dessert."

After hearing a brisk knock, Helga opened the door and warmly greeted the visitor. "Mr. Pfeffer, what a pleasant surprise."

"How nice to see you, as always, Helga," he said as he removed his hat and unbuttoned his coat. "I do not believe I have seen you since that day we met at the—"

"Please forgive me, Mr. Pfeffer. I am hurrying to join the others."

"By all means, go enjoy yourself."

Fredderecke closed the door. "What do you want, Mr. Pfeffer?"

"Mr. Küster, you do not offer to take my coat. Are you not happy to see me?"

"May I take your coat?"

"No, thank you, I will not be long."

Fredderecke offered him a slice of onion pie.

"Thank you, Mr. Küster. I finished my dinner a short while ago. Perhaps Mrs. Küster can wrap a small piece?"

Cäcilia presented Pfeffer a glass fluted pie plate covered with a spotless white kitchen towel. "Please tell Mrs. Pfeffer she may keep the pie plate and the towel."

"This is much too generous, Mrs. Küster." He caressed the smooth glass. "Mrs. Pfeffer and I thank you."

"Has Mrs. Pfeffer been ill? I have not seen her at the market for weeks."

"You are very kind to ask about my wife, Mrs. Küster. We recently discovered we can afford a housekeeper. Our girl comes in three times each week to help Mrs. Pfeffer with her duties. Have you ever had the good fortune to employ a maid, Mrs. Küster?"

"No, I have not." Cäcilia was not envious of Pfeffer's new found wealth because she knew how he had obtained it.

"It is lovely for Mrs. Pfeffer to be relieved of the housework, allowing her time to serve the Party. Perhaps in the future, you and Mr. Küster will experience the happy accident of an inheritance?"

"What do you want, Mr. Pfeffer?" Fredderecke had lost patience with his visitor.

"Mr. Küster, I walk each day for my health. This morning, as I passed your home, I did not see a swastika affixed to a door or window. I thought my eyes were deceiving me. Mrs. Pfeffer noticed my distress and reminded me that you, of course, are very fine people.

"I repeated my morning route after dinner, and I am certain you can imagine my surprise when I saw there was still no swastika. That is when I thought it best to pay Küster a visit. After all, I do not want you to needlessly bring problems on yourselves."

Fredderecke's eyes narrowed. "There must be a mistake. Mrs. Küster and I are conscientious about these things."

"Of that I am certain. That is the reason I am most puzzled about this situation. Mr. Küster, perhaps you would like to see for yourself?"

"I cleaned the windows early this morning—perhaps it fell then." Cäcilia shook the drapes, and a small red flag fluttered to the floor.

"As you can see, Mr. Pfeffer, it was a simple mistake."

"Very good, Mrs. Küster. I should have known better than to question a fine family such as yourselves."

"Think nothing of it, Mr. Pfeffer."

Fredderecke's sarcasm was met by his wife's elbow.

"You are welcome. Mrs. Küster, our maid will return your plate tomorrow. Good night."

છ૭છ૭છ૭છ૭છ૭છ૭

Helga ran as she followed the sounds of screaming until she found a group of Hitler Youth boys smashing plate glass windows of Jewish shops. She picked up a discarded hockey stick and joined them in the night's free-for-all of vandalism and violence. For blocks, she blazed a trail of glistening shards on the sidewalk, which looters used as markers.

At a window filled with expensive pens, her swing was interrupted by the shop owner. Her profuse apologies followed when she noticed the swastika on his lapel pin. Next door, boys in street clothes taunted a man who bravely protected his bakery with a rolling pin. She thought she remembered Haber's Bakery as being owned by a Jew, and the "Closed Saturday" sign propped in the window gave her the peace of mind to leave the boys to their fun.

At midnight, she stood beside a woman whose glasses reflected flames shooting out of a synagogue's cupola. Helga was hypnotized by the orange and red glow, until her trance was broken when a man lifted a little boy onto his shoulders. The child screamed with delight when mist from the fire hoses fell onto his cheeks.

"Ladies and gentlemen," a nearby radio reporter told his listeners, "I stand before the Ada Israel Synagogue as flames reach high into the clear, star-filled sky, and despite the chilly night air, many in the crowd of one hundred or more have unbuttoned their overcoats in the warmth provided by the burning building.

"A few yards from me, firemen protect German roofs from glowing debris jumping out of the flames, and bystanders are shouting down protests from what appears to be the synagogue's rabbi. Another man has joined the fray, but, wait, yes, both men are now lying on the ground.

"Perhaps it is time to hear from someone in the crowd. Miss, may I speak with you?" The reporter approached Helga. "Can you describe for our listeners what is happening on the streets of Nuremberg?"

"It is wonderful." Adrenaline from the electricity in the air made Helga speak too fast for radio. "It is unbelievable. It is incredi—"

"Thank you, miss. Ladies and gentlemen, I see photographers wandering about, and I pray the pictures in the morning newspapers will show you the majesty I see before me."

Helga turned from the reporter to see a man whom she recognized as her family's dentist being prodded with a fireplace poker by a boy who wore a Hitler Youth uniform. She found a discarded cardboard sign with "I Am A Pig" painted crudely on it in white. Her dentist did not raise his head when she dropped the sign around his neck then mercilessly taunted him. The gentle care he had given her family was meaningless in the light of *Kristallnacht*.

"The pig needs dessert. Tie it to a pole."

The boy willingly tied the dentist's arms around a streetlamp.

"Lick the ice cream, Jew," she commanded. "And do not stop until it is all gone."

She and the boy laughed as they watched the poor man lick the cold metal until his tongue split and blood dripped out of his mouth. Satisfied with her handiwork, she strolled home, occasionally pausing to look inside gutted shops. The looters had been thorough, so she was surprised to find Zinsheimer's Jewelry Store intact. She thought about the days when she had dreamed about the special ring a boy would give her someday. During her many visits to the shop, Mr. Zinsheimer had played along with her fantasies and taught her about high-quality diamonds and the difference between fourteen-karat, eighteen-karat, and twenty-four-karat gold.

She shattered the plate glass window with her hockey stick and went inside. Mr. Zinsheimer had taken all the jewelry out of the display cases when the store closed earlier that evening. Frustrated, she pushed aside a curtain, entered the stockroom, and found the safe was locked. She found nothing of value and unleashed her anger on every display case as she left the store.

In the street, Helga weaved around a large crowd who watched another synagogue burn and overheard a woman say, "I simply cannot believe good Germans have done this to those poor Jews."

Confused by the comment Helga approach her and said, "Dear lady, what do you mean 'poor Jews'?"

"Is this not obvious? Good Germans are running through the streets, smashing storefronts and looting. It is a disgrace to the Fatherland."

The obviously well-to-do woman clutched a delicate porcelain vase decorated with hand-painted flowers.

"That is a beautiful vase you are holding, madam. Where did you buy it? I do not know of any German shops that are open this evening."

"Young lady, I see no reason for it to be destroyed."

Chapter 11. Nazi Child

Fredderecke and Cäcilia Küster were average Germans. They had married young, Cäcilia had given birth to their first daughter, Sieglinde, before their first wedding anniversary, and Helga had arrived five years later. As a family they had attended church every Sunday and vacationed every June.

Sieglinde was the happy-go-lucky free spirit in the family. Tall, blue-eyed with naturally light blonde hair that was styled nearly identically to the famous German actress, Renate Müller's. She received high marks in school and studied journalism at the university, which is where she had met her husband, Yossel Veilchenfeld.

Conversely, Helga was stocky, and she wore her dirty-blonde hair in the German traditional braided style. She was as intelligent as her sister, but she took things more seriously and was prone to speaking her mind, a trait that annoyed her parents. When she had discovered the Nazis, she had a sense of belonging that was new to her, and she felt she had finally found her true home.

The Küsters loved both of their children, but Sieglinde was much easier to love.

They had not taken notice of Germany's changing political landscape until Sieglinde married Yossel Veilchenfeld, a Jew whose father was a prominent doctor and whose mother was known for her charity work with the deaf. They loved Yossel and hoped he and his family would stay safe.

Helga's near fanatical interest in the Führer and the Nazis was disturbing to her parents, and they had not supported her involvement in the BDM. Fredderecke had argued with Helga about her political views until he had realized she would not be swayed by reason. He and his wife merely hoped and wished their youngest daughter would change her mind.

CRCRCRCRCRCR

After the final school bell on Monday and Thursday afternoons, eighteen-year-old Helga Küster transformed her secondary school classroom into a Nazi showcase. She covered the walls with posters depicting perfectly Aryan boys and girls demonstrating their love for their Führer and the Fatherland by participating in the many activities organized for the Hitler Youth and BDM, the Hitler Youth for girls. Helga's favorite poster depicted a teenage girl dressed in black shorts and white shirt, drawn in midair as though she were jumping a hurdle, with her head thrown back and one arm pointed straight into the air, out of frame.

Helga washed the chalkboard to keep dust from soiling two huge photos of the Führer, which were separated by an eight-foot-tall, three-foot-wide, red, white, and black Nazi banner. It warmed her to know that he saw deep into her soul, and she stared reverently at the photos. Two flag poles—bearing the Nazi flag on the left and the BDM flag on the right—topped with eagles poised for flight and gripping swastikas in their talons, flanked the chalkboard. Helga checked her watch and took her position by the door.

Sounds of teenage girls talking, laughing, and giggling increased as the rest of the forty members of the club reached the entrance. Helga checked off each girl's name as she passed and noted absences to be investigated.

Inside, the girls jostled for seats, refusing to sit next to that day's rival and quarreling to sit next to that day's best friend.

"Attention! Our leader has arrived."

The room went quiet, save for sounds of bodies snapping to attention and "Heil Hitler!" shouted in unison.

Their leader strode down the aisle between the four rows of chairs and placed a neat pile of papers on the lectern. "Heil Hitler. Let us turn to the flag of our Fatherland and recite our pledge to the Führer."

Each girl thrust her right arm into the familiar Nazi salute. "I swear faithfulness to my Führer, Adolf Hitler. I promise always to render esteem and obedience to him and to the leaders designated by him for me."

"Take your seats."

"Thank you, Helga. Today's topic is 'A Woman's Role in the Third Reich.'

"Our Führer reserves a most special role for women in the Reich. Our duty is to run our household in the German way and to keep our husbands ever ready to do their duty."

Many of the girls were already bored and fought to stay awake. Others listened dutifully, only Helga hung on every word.

"Our role does not stop at serving our brave men, ladies. We are the most important part of fulfilling our dream of creating the master race. Our Führer demands each of us produce as many Aryan children as possible during our fertile years. He created the Cross of Honor of the German Mother, presented personally by him to mothers who produce eight or more children for the Fatherland." She emulated the Führer's stance. "Each of us is bound by a moral responsibility to create a great sea of edelweiss until every German man, woman, and child can remember no other. In one thousand years, our descendants will celebrate our contribution to the Fatherland.

"As you blossom into women, you must give yourselves to the Führer. You are encouraged to—no, you must—bear your first child at the earliest moment in your life. Ignore those who tell you that you must have a husband before bearing a child, for the master race cannot wait."

Helga believed her destiny was to produce soldiers for the Führer. She would go to Berlin, where the Führer would pluck her out of a huge crowd to be his love and mother of his children. Her adolescent body ached for her dream to come true.

"Ladies, you may have been told that bearing a child out of wedlock is shameful or that you will be shunned. Our Führer does not leave you during that time; he provides the unmarried with 'mothers' homes' where you will receive the best care. Once you have given birth, you will receive a stipend until you marry.

"Your parents' outdated ideas have no place in the new Germany, and it is they who will be left behind. The Führer's will is clear and leaves no room for discussion. A master race is not created from old beliefs and stale ideas, it is created by the combined sacrifice of every German."

Helga jumped to her feet and led the zealous ovation of appreciation that swept through the room.

"Ladies, please take your seats. Due to your performance at the Adolf Hitler Regional Games for Boys and Girls in Schrobenhausen two weeks ago, Bund Deutscher Mädel group six-two-two has received an invitation to serve at the Party rally this September."

Helga hugged her clipboard tight against her chest and sighed.

"I am quite pleased that we have served at every rally since 1933, and this year is no exception. Everyone is to do their part for the Führer and the Fatherland. Is that clear?"

The girls' faces glowed with pride and they answered with an enthusiastic, "Yes, *Mädelschaftsführerin.*"

"Ladies, rise and join me in prayer."

> We believe in ourselves as a part of eternity
> as being equal and near to God,
> We believe in ourselves, as the destined links
> in the eternal chain of generations,

We believe in the truth of the National
Socialistic Worldview,
We believe in Adolf Hitler, our eternal
Führer.

"Heil Hitler."

"Heil Hitler, Mädelschaftsführerin."

Helga lingered after the meeting. "Mädelschaftsführerin, I would like to discuss a leadership position. I would like my own BDM group."

"You must stop asking this question. Although your loyalty is unquestioned, you are invaluable at meetings, and your organization skills are impeccable, it is your Jew-loving sister who denies you leadership."

Blinded by hate for her sister, Helga burst into the foyer of her family's home and dropped her books on the small telephone table. "Mother!" she yelled as she ran into the kitchen. "You must have a serious talk with Sieglinde about that Jew."

Cäcilia sighed heavily as she wiped her knife on her apron and dropped freshly chopped onions into a tall pot. "For goodness sake, Helga, must you start the minute you come home?"

"But, Mother, I cannot lead my own BDM group because of my stupid Jew-loving sister and her Jew husband."

"Your father and I did not want you to join that group." Cäcilia placed another onion on the wooden cutting board.

"Sieglinde has ruined my life."

"Stop being dramatic, Helga." Cäcilia's voice sharpened as she wagged the knife toward her daughter. "And you will no longer say such things about your sister or your brother-in-law."

ଔଔଔଔଔଔଔ

The Nazi Party rally, held each September in Nuremburg, was a dazzling spectacle of blind devotion to the Führer. One million Germans made the pilgrimage, and every businessman in the city thanked God for the added marks stuffed into their money clips. Hardened soldiers wept when Hitler led them in solemn ceremonies honoring fallen Nazi heroes, and wild-eyed men and women hailed the Führer from dawn to dusk.

Helga served the Führer by standing behind a steam table. She was envious of the diners, who excitedly chattered about the new stadium and the ceremonies while she plopped overcooked spätzle onto plates brimming with sausages and schnitzel. An old man stopped the line and gushed like a schoolgirl, "What a shame you are stuck here. You are missing a most spectacular rally." Helga held back the desire to plop spätzle onto his shirt.

On the final day of the rally, Helga was beside herself with longing to see the Führer in the flesh. As soon as the dinner rush was over, she ran to the stadium. The moment she saw the magnificent structure, her legs refused to move, her heart fluttered, and her jaw dropped. She was transported to another dimension, an indescribable place where only beauty can survive.

Zeppelin Field was enveloped in more than one hundred fifty blinding light beams climbing hundreds of feet into the air until they disappeared into the heavens with an irresistible supernatural bluish glow. She felt a celestial sense of awe as she stepped through the light and entered a world all its own.

The enormous grandstand, one thousand feet long, was packed with thirty thousand Nazi party officials, high-ranking military officers, and their families. On the field between the grandstand and the spectators' rampart-like concrete bleachers, two hundred thousand fully uniformed soldiers stood at attention while Luftwaffe bombers lumbered by overhead, and pilots in fighter planes buzzed the field or dipped their wings to the crowd. Deafening cheers, magnified by the peoples' endless adulation for the man who replaced the God of their youth, went uninterrupted.

Helga climbed the steep concrete stairs of the spectators' bleachers and pushed her way to the middle of the twenty-third row. She joined spontaneous renditions of *Horst-Wessel-Lied* and her eyes moistened with every verse of *Deutschland Über Alles*. Sweat made her blouse cling to her back, and her hair was soaked with spittle from the fanatics who were higher in the bleachers. She felt her spirit rise out of her when unholy pandemonium broke out at the sight of the man who would lead them to a full realization of the master race. She raised her right arm and screamed above the others, "Heil! Heil!"

The Führer's convertible rolled to a gentle stop at the speaker's podium, where he climbed out and disappeared into the grandstand through a door at ground level. Helga held her breath until he reappeared at the top and began his descent to microphones and motion cameras set up to record his speech for the future, when the master race ruled the world. At the Führer's rostrum, he waited quietly for his worshippers' devotion to peak.

She had never seen the Führer in person. Newspapers and newsreels did not do him justice. It made no difference that he did not physically resemble his vision of the Aryan master race or that Austria was the land of his birth. Emotions whirled through her mind and goose bumps rose on her arms. Waves of hot and cold washed over her as though she had the flu, but in her delirium, she longed for her Führer not for her bed. Her trance broke when he politely covered his mouth and cleared his throat. She followed the unspoken signal and perched on the wooden bench, ready to pounce at the next opportunity to shout "Heil." The pain in her legs and arms from hours of cheers and salutes did not reach her consciousness, nor did her human need for food or drink.

He spoke from a few feet behind the microphones, as if aware that his words may be garbled on the recording if he stood too close. As he spoke, his ever-increasing gesticulations moved Helga to her feet. His rant against the Jews reached its orgiastic peak, and she cheered as loudly as anyone, "Heil! Heil!"

Helga reveled in the afterglow for days.

1939

Chapter 12. Just the Beginning

Jacob and Rose had made their home in a flat a few blocks from Shyke and Pesche when their son, Anshel, had arrived. Rose raised Anshel, while Jacob worked at the bookstore. She and Anshel spent their days playing in the sun and making discoveries that delighted the boy. Insects were Anshel's favorite, and he threw a child's tantrum when his mother forbid him from keeping his newly found friends as pets. The small family was happy, then the Germans invaded Poland.

Awakened by the ringing telephone, Rose rushed to the front room in her bare feet. "Hello?"

"The Germans have invaded Poland!"

"Take a breath, Mama. What are you talking about?" Rose said as she tied the sash on her robe.

"They will be in Kraków soon."

"Stop with your rumors, Mama."

"Do you not understand? We are in danger. We must leave at once."

Anshel got out of bed when he heard Rose talking on the telephone.

"Getting hysterical will not help. Let me talk to Papa."

"We cannot waste time. If we do not leave now, it will be too late."

"Stop crying, you are—"

"Mama, is something wrong?" Anshel pulled on her robe.

"Go back to bed, Anshel. Mama is talking to *Bubbe*."

He jumped and reached for the telephone handset. "Let me talk to Bubbe. I want to talk to Bubbe."

Rose cupped her hand over the mouthpiece. "Not now, Anshel. Go back to bed. And no stomping—we do not want to wake everyone in the building." She turned her attention back to the telephone. "Get hold of yourself, Mama. We will be fine."

"Stop it, Rose, stop it. We must leave immediately—today. You know what they will do to us."

"You are overreacting, as usual. I will call you later; Jacob is awake."

Rose leaned on the bedroom doorjamb and watched Jacob change out of his bedclothes.

"What are you looking at?" Jacob teased. "Who was on the telephone?"

"Mama." Rose folded his pajamas. "She said the Germans have invaded, and she is absolutely hysterical."

"Do not be casual about this, Rose." He buttoned his pants. "We must prepare to leave."

She straightened the bedspread. "Why are you and Mama so gloomy?"

"Have you turned on the radio?" Jacob asked as he tied his shoes.

"Of course not. I did not want to wake you with this nonsense."

"This is not *nonsense*. Those bastards bring nothing but hard times."

He switched on the radio in the front room. As the tubes warmed, panicked, nearly unintelligible words drifted in.

> *The Germans, citing a so-called attack on a small radio station just inside the German border, invaded Poland at dawn. The skies over Warsaw are black with German bombers and citizens are running through the streets searching for safety.*
>
> *Poland was not prepared for this attack, but our heroic Polish army will fight to the last man.*
>
> *Stay tuned for updates throughout the day.*
>
> *God willing, Poland shall not fall.*

Rose set a platter of blintzes on the table. "Eat, Jacob. The Germans will not keep you from your breakfast."

Anshel, still excited from the early morning telephone call, climbed onto his chair. "Mama why did Bubbe call?"

"Bubbe is just being Bubbe." She pointed to his plate. "Eat, dolly, eat."

Rose watched her boy clumsily scoop a bit of food onto a spoon and resisted the urge to guide his little hand. Soon he accidentally found his mouth. "Do not chew with your mouth open, Anshel; it is impolite."

The telephone rang again. Rose heard sobbing before she pressed the receiver against her ear. "Mama, what is it now?"

"Mama, I want to talk to Bubbe. Please, pleeeeeease," Anshel said, rising from his seat.

"Finish your breakfast, Anshel. Mama, you must stop this. I will call you when Jacob leaves." She hung up the telephone more forcefully than she had intended.

"What did your mother say?" Jacob asked.

"The usual, and of course, she refuses to listen to reason."

"It is you who is not listening, Rose."

"Lower your voice, Jacob."

He glanced at his son who was still occupied with a spoon. "You are not a child, Rose. You must pay attention to what is happening around you, if only for Anshel's sake. We must leave Kraków as soon as it can be arranged."

"Jacob, do you want to flee to a country where we know no one and do not speak the language? What would you do in this new country?"

"Poland is no longer safe for us."

"There is no need for this worry." She brushed lint from her husband's overcoat. "By the way, there is no need to hurry home tonight. We are not going to Mama's for Shabbos."

Jacob playfully pinched her cheek. "*That* is good news."

She pretended to be angry and pushed him into the hallway. "You are terrible, Jacob Goldberg."

Now on the kitchen floor, Anshel carefully loaded imaginary dirt into the scoop of his tin dump truck. "Good work today, boys. Tomorrow, we will move rocks," he said to unseen little workers.

Rose knelt next to him and made the proper sound effect as she crashed a toy car into the wall.

"Be careful, Mama, you might hurt the driver!"

"I am sorry, *boychik*."

"That is all right." He picked up the car and wiped it on his pajama pants. "Girls do not know about cars and stuff. Those are boy things."

"You play a few more minutes while I finish the breakfast dishes. We are going to see Bubbe this morning." *Mama is always overreacting. I hope seeing Anshel will bring her to her senses.*

1940

Chapter 13. New Career

In June 1940, Helga was twenty years old and searching for adventure. A help wanted ad in the *Nürnberger Zeitung* promised a career-minded woman good pay and opportunities for advancement at the only concentration camp built exclusively for women: Ravensbrück. She submitted an application letter, and soon after, she found herself in the first row of a small classroom, surrounded by twenty-nine other trainees.

Elke Vogt, the head instructor, had carefully designed the six-week training course to cover every subject from the administrative intricacies of the concentration camp system to prisoner disciplinary techniques. Week one of training was spent on Nazi ideology. This week, week two, Vogt began lessons on what was expected of guards at Ravensbrück, while Helga took detailed notes.

"Trainees, as you are unfamiliar with the inner workings of Ravensbrück, we shall discuss new arrivals, prisoner identification, and your daily duties.

"Prisoners arrive by train at the Fürstenberg depot. Each transport may have one thousand or more prisoners; thus, we must follow these processing procedures for efficiency. One: immediately upon arrival, prisoners disembark. Two: order the prisoners to leave their belongings at the station. Three: line up the prisoners in rows of five. Four: march the column to camp, at double time. Five: upon arrival to the camp, prisoners are registered and released into the general population." She quickly glanced at her students. "Questions?"

Helga raised her hand. "What happens to the bags left behind?"

"Küster, a guard and two prisoners remain at the depot. Bags are loaded onto trucks and transported to camp. The contents are sorted and returned to the German people. Valuables such as jewelry and money are locked up and sent to Berlin. Other questions?"

Elke leaned a poster against the chalkboard and pointed to each colored triangle as she explained the prisoner identification system. "At camp the prisoners are deloused, issued uniforms, and categorized with a triangle sewn onto the uniform. Prisoner's fall into one of the following categories. A red triangle denotes a political prisoner, while green means habitual criminal. Blue means emigrant, and purple means Jehovah's Witness. Pink is reserved for homosexuals, and black is used for asocials—Gypsies, prostitutes, and the like.

"Jewesses are easily identified by an added yellow triangle sewn underneath the first and pointed upward, which creates one of their six-pointed stars.

"After processing, prisoners are marched to their assigned block and released to the *kapo*, a trusted prisoner assigned the task of carrying out orders inside the block. Pay close attention to the following instruction: guards never enter the prisoner blocks. I repeat, guards *never* enter the prisoner blocks. We cannot run the risk of filthy diseases running rampant among the guards. Does anyone have questions about prisoner arrival or identification?"

At Ravensbrück, Helga was among the few volunteer trainees who had an education—most of the women trainees did not and some could barely read. The common thread among all the trainees was the desire to dedicate themselves to the Third Reich and to escape rural living at the same time.

Natascha, who had been born on a dairy farm near the Czech border, asked, "Will you please repeat the part about the triangles, Instructor Vogt? There are so many colors."

Vogt repeated her explanation.

"I am sorry, but I still do not understand. Why are names not sewn on to uniforms, like they do in the Wehrmacht?"

Helga impatiently tapped her pencil on her notebook as the instructor explained the triangles and colors very slowly.

"Instructor Vogt, this still does not make sense to me."

"Perhaps, Natascha, you and I can discuss this after class?"

Finally, Helga thought, *we can move on. That girl is an idiot.*

"I shall now explain *Appell*, roll call, which is conducted twice daily to prevent prisoner escapes. This"—Vogt tapped an enlarged form printed on cardboard with her long wooden pointer—"is the form used to enter the count. There is a line for the number of living prisoners, the number who do not get out of their bunks, and the number of dead since the last roll call."

"How do we know we have counted correctly?" Helga asked.

Vogt pointed to the top left of the form. "Notice the three entries—Block, Count, and Signature—which are completed at the previous count. Yours must match this total."

"What if they do not match?"

"Trainee Küster, if your count does not match the previous, check your addition. If your addition is correct, repeat the count. Do this until the current count matches the last." Vogt looked directly at Natascha. "Does the class have more questions about Appell?"

The rest of the week of training was filled with form after form, which was obviously hard for the semi-illiterates in the class, so Helga volunteered to tutor those who did not understand during evenings and weekends. Vogt was impressed with the trainee who had been attentive and was willing to help the others.

Training concentration camp guards was like military training in that processes, procedures, and regulations were important. The main duty was to keep order among the prisoners and this was not possible with forms alone. After Vogt laid the foundation of the job, she introduced the tools of the trade—weaponry.

Week three brought hands-on weapons training. Vogt issued each trainee an eighteen-inch-long rubber truncheon, the standard for guards, and taught them how to break a prisoner's neck with one blow. Helga was slow to learn the craft, as evidenced by the dozens of women who'd lain in the dirt, moaning as they slowly died.

It was the whip Helga loved, and she learned how to expertly gauge the amount of pain she inflicted with every stroke. At the end of week five, she could rip a prisoner's uniform but never touch the skin, leave a deep bloody gash on a prisoner's arm or leg, and crack her whip within an inch of a prisoner's face. Vogt knew where Helga had been in the camp, based on prisoners' uniforms, the amount of blood present, or the telltale tiny scrape on the tip of the nose left from distance miscalculation.

Week six was saved for pistol training, and Helga could hardly contain herself as the class trotted to the SS firing range two miles from camp. A tingle went down her spine at the first site of the range. Three mounds of dirt, twice as tall as the average man, protected each of the two lanes from ricochets off the concrete bullet traps two hundred feet away.

Vogt led two trainees to the bullet traps and unlocked a metal box. She removed a sheet of heavy white paper printed with the silhouette of a hooked-nose Jew and instructed the trainees how to properly hang targets, then ordered the trainees to stand behind the bullet traps while the others practiced.

Back at the firing line, Vogt gave instructions to the shooters. "There shall be one trainee using each lane, rotating with the others. Once you have stood at the line ten times, you shall rotate with the person behind the bullet trap. We will continue until each of you has acted as a target hanger five times. Separate into two groups. The first to shoot, take your place at the firing line."

Helga pushed her way to the front and took her first practice shot. The target was in no danger as the bullet ricocheted off the concrete. Undeterred, she squeezed off another shot and another until the last bullet in the magazine found the bull's-eye. She went to the back of the queue and was impatient when other trainees took too long to fire their weapons. When it was her turn again, the last trainee's target was untouched, and she could shoot without delay.

"Küster, it appears you are ready for advanced training. *Kapo!*"

The kapo lined up two prisoners in the bullet trap and scurried away.

Helga's first shot caught the female prisoner in the knee, just below the hem of her uniform. Before the prisoner hit the floor, she put seven more holes into the woman. Helga's transformation into a concentration camp guard was complete.

Chapter 14. Mama's Ring

Cruel persecution had become routine in the lives of Kraków's Jews during the first year of German occupation, and the Christian Poles had proven to be as savage as the Germans. Every Jew had learned to be silently grateful when someone else was stopped by a German soldier or a Christian Pole.

In October 1939, Rose had discovered she was expecting her second child. She and Jacob had terrible rows about the pregnancy until it was too late. Tzeitel had been born two months early in May 1940, tiny and fragile. The meager rations the Germans had allowed the Jews was not enough, and Rose produced enough milk for Tzeitel to live but not to thrive. Still, the baby had brought happiness to the family.

Rose carried Tzeitel and kept a close eye on Anshel as they walked to her parents' flat. She slowed to reposition Tzeitel and saw an old woman dance for a German soldier. The woman's long gray hair bounced on her shoulders as the soldier stabbed at her legs until a single bullet ended the woman's humiliation. Anshel pulled at Rose's sleeve and whined, "Mama, Mama, hurry. *Zeyde* is waiting."

When they reached Shyke and Pesche's flat, Anshel ran to his grandfather's side. Months of starvation had stolen Shyke's will to live. His eyes had dark circles and fell deep into their sockets. Anshel was his last joy in life.

Shyke reached out a bony, wrinkled hand and stroked the child's face. "Boychik, when I am gone, stay strong for your sister."

"Zeyde," Anshel sobbed, "I will always take care of Tzeitel."

"Papa, do not say such things," Rose scolded her dying father. "You will see Anshel become a man."

"No, Rose, I will not live to be with him at his bar mitzvah."

Pesche pulled Rose away. "Do not give your father false hope."

"Mama, he must not die."

Pesche sat on the worn sofa and patted a cushion that had been turned over to hide the upholstery worn through to the stuffing. "Death would be a blessing."

"Do not say that, Mama."

"I only say what is true." Pesche reached into her apron pocket and laid a ring onto Rose's palm. A *chai*, the Hebrew symbol for life, was engraved inside the band.

"Mama, what a beautiful ring."

"My mother, Golde, fell in love with my father, who was the poorest man in the shtetl. Golde's mother did not want the marriage. She refused to believe her daughter could love such a man. After they married, they were still poor, but very happy. My father, Elya, wanted to go to Kraków to find his fortune. Golde dutifully agreed, and the day they left the shtetl, your great-grandmother gave this ring to her daughter and said, 'Golde, this has been passed down from mother to oldest daughter for generations. It is what ties our past to our future. Do not tell Elya; he will be tempted to sell it during lean times.'"

"Mama, why are you telling me this?"

"Hush. I did not know this until soon before my mother died." Pesche closed Rose's fingers around the ring. "I give this to you now. You will know what to do with it. But do not tell Jacob. Men are weak."

"Mama, I cannot take the ring. It is not time."

"This is best. Your papa and I will not live to see the Germans leave Kraków."

Rose slipped the ring into her pocket. "I swear that I will keep the ring safe until this is all over—then I will give it back to you."

"From your mouth to God's ears. It is late, and you must go. You cannot break curfew."

ଔଔଔଔଔଔ

"Jacob, stop pacing."

"It has been over a year since the Germans confiscated our radio and shut down the newspapers. What am I supposed to do, Rose?"

"Please, sit. I have a surprise."

"If this is another baby, Rose," he said as he settled into the chair, "I swear, you *will* visit the midwife."

"No." She sat on his lap and wrapped his arm around her waist. "I took the children to see Mama today."

"How is your father holding up?"

"No worse than anyone else."

"And your mother?"

"She still thinks the Germans will be here forever."

"You should listen to her."

"Please, Jacob, I do not want to argue." She playfully searched her pockets, and with great ceremony, laid Mama's ring on her open palm.

"My God, Rose, where did you get this?" He held up the ring and watched as the dim light danced off the diamonds.

She squeezed his neck and put her head on his shoulder. "It was my grandmother's, who gave it to my mother, and now I will pass it on to our little Tzeitel."

"The ring itself is worth one, maybe two months of food on the black market. But if I sell the gold and diamonds separately"—he carefully inspected the ring from all angles—"I would probably get enough food for three weeks with the big diamond alone. The two smaller ones could bring another month, and the gold, well, since it is fourteen-karat, it must be worth another month. Tomorrow, I will—"

"Absolutely not." She snatched the ring. "This is Tzeitel's ring and that is all there is to it."

"What are you, Rose, crazy?"

"Lower your voice. Do you want the neighbors to hear you?"

"Get off me."

She slid from his lap.

Jacob paced and rubbed his forehead. "We must be practical."

"No, this is for Tzeitel."

"Listen to me. If we do not feed our children, they will die. Do you understand that, Rose? The children will die!"

A neighbor banged on the wall.

"Shut up and mind your own business!"

"Jacob, please, be quiet."

"We finally have something valuable enough to buy food for our children and you want to keep it?"

The neighbor banged again.

"Stop that, dammit! I told you to mind your own damn business."

Rose pulled his arm. "Sit down, and we will talk about this as adults."

He shook himself loose. "Anshel is wasting away, and you barely make enough milk for Tzeitel. With this we can feed the children. How can you not understand?"

"I will not take my daughter's birthright away from her."

"Rose, if we do not buy food, it will not matter to Tzeitel or anyone else."

"You cannot talk like that!" she screamed.

Jacob's slap sent her to the floor. "We will not die because you are living in a fantasy world."

She rubbed her cheek. "If you ever do that again, I will . . . "

"What, Rose? What will you do?"

"I will take the children to my mother's."

"For God's sake, we must eat."

Rose looked up into Jacob's eyes. "Not at Tzeitel's expense. I will never part with Mama's ring."

"But, Rose . . . "

"Never."

1941

Chapter 15. To the Ghetto

The sun rose over Kraków's Jewish Quarter as soldiers beat on doors with their rifle butts, barking, "*Raus, raus!*" Christian Poles who assisted the German soldiers often lingered after a flat was vacated and helped themselves to whatever caught their eyes.

The heavy wooden door to Rose and Jacob's flat broke open, and Anshel cried out, "Papa! Papa!"

Rose pulled a blanket to her chin as a Pole eyed her with a sly grin. "All Jews are resettling in Podgórze, except you. We will get better acquainted." He sneered at Jacob. "Pack one suitcase each. Be ready in five minutes, or you will be shot."

Jacob stuffed four bags with clothing and sat on top of them to close the latches. He put the bags in the hallway, pried a blue and white ceramic mezuzah from the doorjamb, and smashed it on the floor. Rose dressed herself, but there was no time to dress the children. Anshel was still wearing pajamas and Tzeitel only a diaper when the family joined the rest of the Jews in the street.

The Germans chose Szeroka Street as the gathering place. The area between the Old Synagogue and a small park had been the Jewish Quarter's heart. Shops lined both sides of the street, and the cobblestones had welcomed all for centuries. Women used to dress in their best clothes to meander through the square, while couples fell in love in the restaurants and children ran every which way, laughing as adults chided them for one silly thing or another.

The German officer commanding the roundup wandered through the crowd and demanded ransom in exchange for life. When he reached Rose and Jacob, his uniform jacket pockets bulged to overflowing, and he was forced to hand payments to an aide.

"Jew, what will you pay for your family's life?"

Rose held her breath. *Stay quiet, Jacob, please stay quiet.*

Jacob reached into his pocket. "We have a—"

A man behind Jacob held up a fat leather wallet. "I have money."

The officer forgot about Jacob and handed the wallet to his aide. "The mint never stops printing money, does it? Let us get on with it. You have your orders."

The aide gestured with his rifle. "All of you, under the tree. Make a line with your backs to me."

Fifteen men of all ages, shapes, and social statuses stood side by side. The aide checked his pistol for bullets and shot each man at point blank range.

The officer then shouted. "Get up, Jews. It is to the ghetto with you."

Rose stood on her toes and tried to see over the crowd. "Jacob, I cannot find Mama and Papa. We must be with them."

"Come, Rose, we must go. We will find them later."

"Jews, march."

The group of Jews marched away from the streets they had occupied for hundreds of years. Rose glanced back as she stepped out of Kraków's Jewish Quarter for the last time and saw the bodies strewn about the square. As the crowd moved past the Old Synagogue, she saw her parents lying together on the sidewalk. Both of them had bullet holes in their foreheads.

The square, emptied of its former inhabitants, looked sad and disheveled. Items too heavy to carry were strewn about. Fragments of glass—from windows broken during the roundup—were sparkling happily in the sun. Rose's anger flared at the sun, which still danced on Szeroka Street.

Anshel heard adults curse at the soldiers through clenched teeth. The words were unfamiliar to him, but he instinctively understood their meaning. He pulled his arm from his mother's tight grip and used his hands as a megaphone. "*Petzl.*"

"Anshel, we do not use those words."

"Leave him be, Rose," Jacob said. "He will hear worse before this is over."

Some Poles watched the parade, while others turned down side streets to walk blocks out of their way to avoid their own discomfort. A tram waited for the tracks to clear, and the driver screamed that the Germans were not moving the Jews along fast enough.

They crossed the Vistula River and stopped at Zgody Square in Podgórze, the poorest area of Kraków.

"This is madness," Jacob shouted. "We cannot stand here like sheep, oblivious to the wolf stalking them. There are no more than fifty of them, and we are thousands."

"Hush."

"No, Rose, I cannot stand what I see here. We must revolt!"

The rabbi from the Old Synagogue took Jacob's arm. "Lower your voice, young man. We cannot overtake them."

"Rabbi, they cannot kill every one of us."

"So, they have taken us from our homes. Once we are settled, they will leave us alone. There is nothing more they can do to us, but we can pray."

"Then I will attack them myself. I will not let them think we are cowards."

Anshel pulled on his father's coat sleeve and said, "Papa, I am thirsty."

Jacob's resolve to revolt melted away.

ଔଔଔଔଔଔ

"Jews, each flat shall accommodate four families. Find your new home."

In the mayhem, Aaron Wislicki, a Jewish judge who lived outside the city, protested. "This is quite enough, young man. We have followed orders, but this is too much. You expect me and my wife to live in a flat with another family? That is preposterous."

"You are no longer a king, Jew."

"Young man, I do not think, nor have I ever thought that I am a king. My wife and I simply do not belong with the others. I demand you rectify our living situation at once."

"You want me to *rectify your living situation*, Jew?"

"You heard me."

Rose heard a rifle blast before she felt a piece of Aaron's skull hit her cheek.

"And does the Jew's wife want a similar living situation?"

"Mama"—Anshel squeezed her hand—"I promise I will take care of you and Papa."

Rose looked deep in his eyes and saw an understanding that was far beyond what any child had a right to possess.

Everyone rushed through the new ghetto, and Jacob led his family to a building far from the front gate. Inside, they climbed three flights to find a flat with enough room for them.

"Hello, my name is Jacob Goldberg. This is my wife, Rose, and our children, Anshel and Tzeitel."

A man stopped tightening the rope that ran down the middle of the large room and shook Jacob's hand. "Welcome. I am Melek Shamir. The sheets are meant to give each family a bit of privacy. There are ten others in the bedroom, and with me and your four, we are now fifteen living here. I expect a few more will join us." He pointed to the large window overlooking the courtyard. "Jacob, you take the window. Your children need sunlight."

A fat woman dressed in a floor-length mink coat covering four layers of expensive clothing, rushed in from the hallway and straight to the window. "This will not do, Reuben. It is not southern exposure. I must get three hours of sunlight every day. Reuben, you must find another flat. It must have southern exposure and"—she sniffed the air—"no odor."

"Miriam, this is the only flat we can find that still has room for us. You will spend time outdoors. For now, we stay here." Reuben Gomulka owned the steel mill outside Kraków. Nothing had changed for him until a week earlier, when a German walked into his office and announced the steel mill was German property.

Melek said. "Welcome, Mr. Gomulka, how nice to see you again."

Reuben searched Melek's face. "You look familiar."

"I was a blacksmith at your mill."

"Our bags are in the hall. Fetch them—I want to get settled."

Melek gritted his teeth. "Mr. Gomulka, I no longer work for you. Get the bags yourself."

"The whole world has gone mad when a *blacksmith* speaks to me like that. Do not expect your job to be waiting when this is over.

Melek raised his fist.

Jacob stopped him. "It is not worth it."

Miriam Gomulka pushed Rose away from the window. "No, no, no, I need sunlight and Reuben cannot sleep without fresh air."

Jacob bowed slightly. "Miriam? Melek and I have discussed the arrangements. In deference to my children, my family will stay near the window."

Reuben demanded Jacob's name.

"Jacob Goldberg. And yours?"

"You may refer to me as Mr. Gomulka. See here, Goldberg—"

"Reuben, you may call me Mr. Goldberg."

Melek suppressed a laugh.

"Mr. Goldberg, we will not live in these horrible conditions without a modicum of fresh air. Move your things at once."

"Reuben, you will take your place by the door."

"Listen here, Goldberg."

Melek moved toward Reuben. "You will address my friend as *Mister* Goldberg."

Reuben dragged his bags just inside the door. "Come, Miriam, it is easier to leave the flat from here."

"But, Reuben, you know how I feel when I do not get enough sunlight."

"Miriam, we stay here. And take that ridiculous coat off."

Melek hung the last sheet. "The Germans will not ration enough food for anyone, especially the children. Oh, yes, and of course, Miriam, it might be best to pool our resources."

Miriam poked her husband's side to prod him to her defense. He said nothing.

"That is a good idea," said Jacob, digging into Anshel's bag. "We have a little money, a hundred zlotys, and Rose has gold earrings and a bracelet. We will add our wedding rings."

Rose looked at the sky through the hard-won window. *Thank you, God. Jacob did not mention Mama's ring.*

Melek added his gold to the pile. "Reuben, what did you and your wife bring?"

"Miriam and I did not feel it necessary to bring valuables."

"You and Miriam brought nothing?"

"If you and Mr. Goldberg will assist my wife and myself, I will happily pay you double when this is all over."

"Hah." Rose could not contain herself.

Jacob smirked.

"You want us to feed you and your fat wife on the promise that you will pay us later?" Melek asked.

"That is correct. This is quite a good deal for you and, of course, for Mr. Goldberg."

"Fuck. You."

Reuben's voice quivered. "We may have a trinket or two."

Melek straightened a sheet. "Yes, Reuben, you may want to see if you can find a *trinket or two*."

Reuben found the watch and chain his father had given him on his bar mitzvah, three gold bracelets, a diamond brooch with matching earrings, and a pair of ivory cufflinks.

"Will this be sufficient to feed us, Mr. Shamir?"

"Yes. For now."

"And it goes without saying that as I have made the largest contribution, Miriam and I will be allotted larger portions."

Melek straightened another sheet. "Do I have to repeat myself, Reuben?"

"No, sir. We share equally."

Chapter 16. More Death

The Germans had crammed thousands of Jews into old tenement buildings. Within weeks, the aged plumbing broke down and little effort was made to repair it. Occasionally, water trickled out of taps, but it was impossible to bathe or wash clothes. Without proper sanitation, disease born from filth rampaged through the ghetto, but doctors were forbidden basic medical supplies.

Jacob took a last look at his tiny daughter before he went to sleep. There were no longer curtains on the window—Rose had improvised a coat for Anshel—and he saw Tzeitel was naked. "Rose, where is her diaper?"

"It is hanging up here. It was not dry when I put her to bed. We only have one diaper and the poor thing has dysentery." She pulled the dried cloth diaper from the curtain rod and looked around for a diaper pin. "Miriam is still complaining about the smell, Jacob."

"Too hell with Miriam Gomulka."

"I have every right to complain about that awful smell, Mr. Goldberg," Miriam said through the improvised room divider.

He pulled back the sheet and looked her in the eye. "But you do not have a heart."

Taken aback, Miriam said, "Well, I never . . . "

"Of course not." Rose appeared next to Jacob. "You never thought of anyone but yourself. You never had a kind word. You never did anything to help another human being."

"Now, Mrs. Goldberg, that is quite enough."

Rose walked toward Miriam. "No one has ever told you the truth, have they, Miriam?"

Miriam backed up until she was against the door.

"Miriam, I will tell you the truth. You are an evil, evil woman. You would rather starve a child than miss even one morsel of food. Look at you"—she pointed at Miriam's dress—"your clothes still fit. My dress hangs on me as though I were a hanger in the closet.

"There is no one in this horrible place who deserves to be here, except you. I keep asking myself why you are not dead yet. What is your secret to staying alive, Miriam Gomulka?"

Rose and Miriam stared at each other until Jacob gently tugged Rose's arm. "I have something much more important than you to tend to, Miriam."

Jacob put his arms around his wife. "Darling, I know she is a terrible person, but we have no choice but to live with her."

Rose felt the bones of his chest against her cheek, and she pulled away. "Tzeitel needs her diaper."

As she lifted Tzeitel's legs, they felt heavy and cold to the touch. Rose ran her finger across Tzeitel's forehead, then wrapped the child tightly in a tattered blanket.

"Rose, I will take her downstairs to wait for the funeral wagon."

"No, Jacob. She needs her mother."

Tears ran down Rose's face as she carried her dead baby to the street. Soon, the funeral wagon stopped, and she tenderly placed Tzeitel beside another child to be buried in a mass grave outside the ghetto.

1942

Chapter 17. Consequence

Every night, Sieglinde went to the beer halls to forget about the emptiness in her life without her Yossel.

"Gimme another one," Sieglinde said to the hostess.

"Go home, miss. This is no place for you."

"No, bitch, I said I want beer."

The waitress pushed Sieglinde toward the door. "You should go home."

"Shuddup. Gimme beer."

Conrad Pfeffer, who was at the beer hall celebrating his latest windfall, went to the stumbling young woman. "Miss, are you Helga Küster's sister, Sieglinde?"

"Why do you care, fat pig?"

"That is just the beer talking, Sieglinde. Come, meet my friends." He gently took her arm and guided her to a long wooden table surrounded by men waving their ceramic beer steins and singing army songs.

He lifted her onto the table and nuzzled her neck. "You should not be out alone. Someone could take advantage of you."

"Who cares? It is all a lie. The great Thousand-Year Reich. Hah."

"You do not mean that," he said as he slipped his hand under her skirt and up her thigh.

"Get away from me, Nazi." She jumped off the table. "'Heil Jackass. Heil Jackass.'"

Laughter spurred her on, and she goose-stepped drunkenly to the stage.

She raised her arms to quiet the hall. "We must all be perfect Aryans. Look at me! I am your Führer and the model Aryan. My black hair is perfectly blond." She posed like a model. "My chiseled features and muscular body are what you all must aspire to. And the best part, my fellow Germans, I am not even one of you. I was born in Austria!"

Pfeffer offered his hand to assist her from the stage. "Sieglinde, come with me. I have another friend who would very much like to meet you."

Sieglinde was too drunk and tired to protest as he led her to the Palace of Justice. The night guard hoisted Sieglinde over his shoulder and carried her to a holding cell. When he returned, he handed Pfeffer a receipt.

"Here," the guard said, "you can cash this in tomorrow. It must be your lucky day, Pfeffer. All the guys in the back are quite smitten with her and agree that the price for a drunk, pretty young woman just went up."

Pfeffer folded the receipt and shoved it into his jacket pocket. "I am always happy to help."

Chapter 18. Going Home

Helga had been granted a thirty-day pass and looked forward to a long rest. She carried the letter from Conrad Pfeffer, in which he promised to share the generous reward he received when he delivered Sieglinde to the Gestapo. The letter from her mother, full of worry about her eldest daughter's unknown fate, lay in a wastebasket back at camp.

"How may I help you, miss?" The stationmaster asked as he approached from behind the caged ticket window.

"I would like a ticket to Nuremberg, please."

"Through Hamburg or Berlin? The Hamburg route is scenic, but the route through Berlin has a three-hour layover, and there would be time to enjoy the city. The travel time for either route is approximately the same. Which would you prefer, miss: the scenic route or time to visit Berlin?"

"Hamburg, please."

"The next train to Hamburg is scheduled to depart at three o'clock this afternoon. However, a train was due yesterday and should be here in a few minutes. Once it is unloaded and hosed out, it will depart, and the passenger train can come into the station. The delay should not be more than an hour. I apologize for the inconvenience."

"How much does a coach ticket cost?"

"Twelve marks."

She paid, and he slid a first-class ticket under the cage. "To make up for the delay."

Helga sat on a bench overlooking the tracks. A steam locomotive pulled into the station, and five SS soldiers cracked jokes as they slid the doors open on the four cattle cars, which were perfectly aligned on the platform. Women tumbled over one another to the cement, much to the soldiers' delight. Prisoners were ordered to toss the bodies of women who had died on the journey onto the platform.

She called to the officer in charge. "Lieutenant, it could be fun to give your men a challenge."

"We are on a schedule, and a passenger train is waiting a few miles back. What do you have in mind?"

"A little recreation will not cause a long delay. Let us see how fast they can load and unload the cars. One man per car. Whoever is fastest after ten rounds, wins."

"And the prize, miss?"

"The pride of victory."

"The cars were loaded with approximately the same number of prisoners in each. However, I am afraid that discrepancies in the number of dead will give some men an advantage."

"In that case, Lieutenant, include the corpses."

With the rules set, Helga started the first round. "On your mark. Ready. Set. Go."

Floors slick with urine, feces, vomit, and blood made it hard for the weak prisoners to climb back into the cattle cars. The soldiers affixed bayonets to their rifles and stabbed at the women to clear the platform. They soon realized adding corpses each round reduced their chances of winning, and they switched to beatings with clubs and rifle butts.

"Well done, men"—the lieutenant applauded—"you have all won. Tonight, the first round is on me!"

Helga shook the officer's hand. "Thank you, Lieutenant. I have not had this much fun in months."

ଔଔଔଔଔଔ

The day after Sieglinde disappeared, Fredderecke and Cäcilia discovered she was taken to Gestapo headquarters. The SS man at the information desk had told them Sieglinde was scheduled to be transferred to a concentration camp but did not know when or to which one. They had looked forward to Helga's visit and hoped she could help them find Sieglinde.

"Helga will be here soon, Fredderecke." Cäcilia wrung her hands as she paced.

Fredderecke sat in his favorite chair and balanced an unfolded newspaper on his lap. "Why do you even want her to visit?"

"The Gestapo may give *her* more information."

"You are dreaming, Cäcilia." He snapped open the newspaper and pretended to read.

When she heard the front door open, Cäcilia took a deep breath and said, "She is here."

The family reunion was stilted. Cäcilia hugged Helga, and Fredderecke said words a father would say to his child who has been long absent. There was inconsequential small talk until evening.

"Are you aware that your sister has yet to come home?"

Helga took a sip of coffee, and as she set her cup on a saucer, she said, "Have you found out where she ran off to, Mother?"

Fredderecke balled his fist. "How dare—"

"—Fredderecke, stop. Read the paper while Helga and I talk alone."

He glared at his daughter and left his wife to her hopes.

"She was taken to Gestapo headquarters, and they will not tell us why she was arrested or where she is. We hoped you might be able to find out more."

"I do not have influence with the Gestapo."

"Please, Helga, we are desperate."

Disgusted by her mother's plea, she said. "What is done is done. But I will go to Gestapo headquarters in the morning. Will that make you happy, Mother?"

"Thank you, thank you, Helga." Cäcilia shed tears of relief.

"Mother, why are you so interested in the getting Sieglinde back? She was just a Jew-lover."

Cäcilia measured her words for fear that Helga would refuse her request. "She is your sister, and she loves you very much."

"Why did she marry that Jew? You must not forget that the Jew left her and never even said 'goodbye.'"

Fredderecke stood near the kitchen door and listened.

Cäcilia's blood ran cold. "You have no heart, Helga. You readily choose cruelty over kindness, hate over love. I can feel it down to my bones that you are behind Yossel's disappearance." Cäcilia's face was contorted with fear. "I despise you and everything you hold dear."

"Cäcilia! Do not you say things you will regret." Fredderecke said.

"Please, Helga"—Cäcilia fell to her knees—"you promised to go to Gestapo headquarters to ask about her. We do not want you to do anything. We only want to know where your sister is."

ଓଓଓଓଓଓଓ

As Helga stood near the door of Gestapo headquarters, she felt sure of the decision she made after her mother's disgusting display the night before— Jew-lovers were no better than Jews. Before she entered Gestapo headquarters, she stopped to read the list of violations Fredderecke and Cäcilia had committed. The list was arranged chronologically with detailed descriptions of each violation written neatly beside each date. Inside the building, she climbed the familiar marble stairs and took her place at the end of the short line of men and women awaiting their turn to speak with an officer. She waited nearly thirty minutes before she was called.

"Next," the officer said as he waved Helga to his desk.

"Heil Hitler."

His demeanor was businesslike. "Offense."

"Jew sympathies."

"Jew blood?"

"Sympathies."

"I do not hear that one often these days. I have to find the right form." He went to a filing cabinet by the window. The top drawer was full of forms arranged in alphabetical order. "Johann, where is the form for Jew sympathies?"

"We ran out of those a while back. Use the traitor form."

The soldier pulled the form titled "Traitor" from the drawer and rolled it into his typewriter. "Your name?"

"Helga Küster."

"Name of traitor?"

"Fredderecke and Cäcilia Küster."

"Two? We have to do them one at a time."

"Fredderecke. The surname is—"

"I have the surname. Address?"

Helga gave him the information.

"Nature of offense."

"Jew sympathies."

He typed up the rest of the form and pulled it out of the typewriter.

"You do not want to know more?"

"Nobody cares. Just sign at the bottom. The next one is the same complaint, correct? What is the name?"

"Cäcilia. C-Ä-C-I-L-L-I-A."

He copied the rest of the information from the form bearing Fredderecke's name. "Sign here. I will give you one voucher for both. If the cashier has any questions, tell him to see me. Heil Hitler."

Helga cashed in the voucher and headed for the Nuremberg train station.

"Excuse me, sir. I have a reservation to Kraków next week, but I would like to leave today."

"May I see your ticket?" The clerk scratched his chest. "Miss, your ticket is for the night train. The ticket for the day train to Kraków adds fifty marks to the price."

"Fifty marks! That is robbery, sir."

"It is wartime, miss. The railroads incur extra expenses when the tracks are bombed. Do you want the ticket or not?"

"I want to upgrade to first class."

"First class is another twenty-five marks,"

Helga was grateful for the extra money she got from denouncing her parents and handed the clerk seventy-five marks.

"Here you are, miss. The train to Kraków leaves in ten minutes from track 14."

She hurried to the train and found the first-class passenger car. The conductor confirmed her ticket and led her to her compartment, where she settled in and waited for departure. Soon, a young man in an SS uniform appeared at Helga's compartment door. "Excuse me, miss, may I join you? There has been a mix up with my ticket and the compartment I was assigned to is full."

Helga nodded her permission. The man was six feet tall, his blond, slicked back hair reflected the dim lighting, and his eyes were the kind of deep blue that made women all over Germany melt into his arms.

"Thank you, miss." He stuffed his second-class ticket into his trousers and sat next to Helga on the brown leather seat. In his most seductive voice, he purred, "Are you going to leave me at the Berlin stop or will I have the pleasure of your company all the way to Kraków?"

"Kraków," she stammered.

"Pardon?"

Her throat was tight. "Um, I am traveling to Kraków."

"Are you traveling for business or leisure? Forgive me, where are my manners? I am Günther Baumgartner. And you are . . . ?"

A warmth slowly radiated through her body. "Helga Küster. I have a new position at Auschwitz."

"What a happy coincidence," Günther said, smiling, "so do I."

"I s-s-see. What do you do?"

He leaned in closer. "Enough about me. Tell me about Helga Küster."

She felt the blush in her cheeks and in her embarrassment, nudged him away. "No, please, tell me more about Auschwitz."

"I have served the Fatherland in many capacities. When I joined, I was assigned to the Führer's bodyguard unit."

"How thrilling that must have been."

"You cannot imagine how kind and generous the Führer is to his staff."
That prick would not be "kind" *or* "generous" *with a gun to his head,*
Günther thought.

Love for the Führer oozed from Helga's every pore. "I knew that he
would be."

"I have an interesting, if slightly embarrassing, story of how I was
assigned to my new prestigious unit. My mother was afraid, as any German
mother is, of the danger of being so close to the Führer. She reached the
Führer by telephone, and she begged him to transfer me from his bodyguard
unit. I still do not know how she did that.

"He said, 'Mrs. Baumgartner, I shall personally transfer your son to a
less dangerous assignment. I cannot have a German mother angry with
me.'"

"I wish *I* could speak with him. Then what happened?"

Does this idiot really think the Führer would take a call from somebody's
mother? "We happened to be at the Berghof, and the very next day, the
Führer's chauffeur drove me to a concentration camp outside Munich in the
black Mercedes the Führer uses on weekends."

"Such an honor! It is almost unbelievable."

"You cannot imagine. To continue, the commandant at Dachau
concentration camp took a special interest in me, and I was soon promoted
to a position where I oversaw all the guards."

"Oh, Günther!"

"Yes, but again my mother stepped in. She felt I was too far away from
her and arranged for a transfer to the *Einsatzgruppen*."

"What is that?"

"We travel the countryside and arrest partisans and other enemies of the
Reich. My unit was assigned to Lithuania. You can imagine what that was
like in the winter. So, long story short, I asked to be transferred back to the
concentration camp system. I am so happy I did, too, because here I am,
riding first class on the train with a lovely young woman."

"Why Auschwitz?"

"Because I knew that I would meet a girl just like you, my dear. Enough
about me"—Günther cupped her chin—"tell me about you."

She talked nonstop to Berlin, during the forty-five-minute layover, then
all the way to Kraków. Günther fought valiantly to stay awake as she droned
on with her tedious story. He was the happiest man in the world when the
train stopped in Kraków.

"Where are you staying tonight, Helga?"

"Near Szeroka Street."

"What luck! I am to meet a friend in that area. Let me accompany you to your hotel."

"That would be a pleasure, Günther. The hotel is approximately two kilometers from here. Perhaps we should take a taxi."

"I am sorry, my dear, please forgive me. I seem to have misplaced my wallet in Berlin. The evening is so crisp; a walk will be good for us."

"That is bad luck. I can pay for a taxi. I do not mind."

"If you do not mind, then a taxi to your hotel will be most welcome."

Helga paid for the ride before she and her handsome companion opened the car door in front of the hotel. The soldiers who filled the outdoor café would be ruthless with their jokes if they discovered Günther had taken charity from a woman.

Lies and bigger lies flew from table to table amid laughter and lighthearted demands for more drinks and food from the Polish waiters. Helga followed Günther through the crowd to the bar.

"How can it be? Ludwig? I have not seen you in ages, my friend."

Ludwig slammed his glass of beer on the bar and rose to greet the man he knew from his days at Dachau.

"Günther!"

The men slapped each other on the back as they shook hands, while they made the usual small talk about the weather and army food.

"And who have we here, Günther?"

"Forgive my manners. This is my new friend, Helga Küster. Helga, this is Ludwig von Waechter. He and I were comrades at Dachau."

Ludwig glanced at Günther with knowing approval as his lips lightly brushed Helga's hand.

"Excuse me, Günther, I must powder my nose."

"Do not be long, my dear. I miss you already."

"Where did you find that one? She is not your usual type."

"She let me sit with her in first class, Ludwig. I owe her a little bit of attention."

ଔଓଔଓଔଓଔଓ

The following morning, Helga and Günther rode the tram to the Kraków train depot, where she bought two first-class tickets for the short journey to Auschwitz, despite Günther's feeble attempt to stop her from purchasing his. A wooden boxcar was pulled up next to their passenger train. They could hear shouts and see arms thrusting out of the small barbed wire window near the top of the boxcar as prisoners offered bracelets, necklaces, and watches for a sip of water or a morsel of food. Passengers milling around the station pretended not to hear.

"Do not bother about that, Helga."

"Do they have no shame? That window should be boarded up, if for no other reason than to keep them from embarrassing themselves."

Soon, the train slowly pulled out of the station, then stopped when it cleared the canopy, where it changed tracks and backed up. A railroad worker coupled the wooden boxcar to the train, and the journey to Auschwitz began.

As they disembarked at the Auschwitz train station, Helga glanced back. "Do they never shut up? They sound like stray cats." She unfolded a small map and ran her finger from the depot to the camp. "It is only a kilometer or so, shall we walk?"

"The bags are heavy. I would be happy to pay for a taxi, but . . . "

"I will pay."

"That is most gracious, Helga. Perhaps you could give me the fare now. I do not want the taxi driver to think I cannot pay my own way."

When they arrived at camp, Günther paid the driver and retrieved their bags. Beneath the iron *Arbeit Macht Frei* ("Work Sets You Free") sign spanning the camp entrance, an SS soldier confirmed their orders and lifted the gate.

At the camp's main road, a man wearing a striped, pajamalike uniform and a woman wearing a dress made from matching cloth, shuffled by on the muddy path and did not greet the new guards.

"Jew-swine, stand at attention," Günther said. "Remove your cap."

The man's cap hit his thigh with a loud crack. "I am sorry, sir. I did not see you. Please forgive me, sir."

Helga joined in. "Where are you going, *Scheissbeutel*?"

"Madam, Dr. Mengele sent for this woman to—"

"—woman? The only woman I see is my lovely friend." Günther flashed his gleaming smile at Helga. "*You*," he said to the prisoner, "Jew-dog, are walking a pig."

"Yes, sir, I am walking a pig, sir."

The Germans wanted a sterilization method to ensure annihilation of Jews and other enemies of the state. Experimentation with X-rays showed promise, although women often got burns that did not heal. The woman standing before Helga had received high doses of radiation two weeks prior. Her wounds had become gangrenous, and pus oozed through the coarse cloth of her dress.

"Why do you not keep yourself clean, pig?"

"Madam, the doctor sent for me, madam."

"That is no answer." Helga pointed to stairs leading to the door on a block behind the prisoners. "Pig, get on your escort's back. Shitbag, hop up the stairs. When you reach the top, I will order you to hop down or jump."

The prisoner hopped up to the landing and turned to Helga.

"Jump."

He fell. His blood drained into the gravel, the woman still clinging to him.

"Get up, pig. Do not keep the good doctor waiting."

Helga and Günther headed for the commandant's office to finish their paperwork and receive their first assignments at Auschwitz.

C3CRCRCRCRCR

Fredderecke and Cäcilia had realized their beloved Sieglinde would never return. Neither had admitted to the other the relief they had felt the day before, when Helga had ended her visit early—that would have made their contempt for their youngest child real. Their hearts ached as they sat quietly, Fredderecke reading the newspaper and Cäcilia darning socks, each inside their own thoughts, until they heard someone pound on the front door.

"Gestapo. Open up."

Fredderecke's mouth went dry and Cäcilia froze.

The pounding on the door got harder and louder.

"Cäcilia, go into the bedroom and hide."

"I stay with you."

"Gestapo. Open up. Now."

Fredderecke pushed his wife toward the bedroom. "No, Cäcilia, save yourself."

The door gave way and two men entered. They were nondescript and in other circumstances would be accountants or teachers. But their uniforms made them terrifying.

"Fredderecke Küster?"

"Yes."

"The Gestapo has been informed that you are a Jew."

Fredderecke's mind swirled with fragments of thoughts mixed with fear and confusion. "I am not a Jew."

"That is not the information we have been given."

"But, I do not understand, sir. Why do you—"

"You and your wife are to accompany us to headquarters for questioning," the agent said as he handcuffed Fredderecke's wrists and pulled him outside.

Cäcilia said nothing as she was shoved into the backseat of the waiting car, next to her husband. She saw a tear roll down his cheek and knew they would never see one another again.

Chapter 19. Death and Food

Reuben and Miriam Gomulka had once lived in a twelve-room house at the edge of Kraków. Their sunroom had overlooked the perfectly manicured garden where their dogs had played. For twenty years, a lovely Polish woman had taken care of their home, and the first sign of the inconveniences to come was when the Germans had forced them to fire her. They had adjusted to the ever-increasing restrictions until the humiliation of living in squalor in the ghetto, which was almost more than they could bear.

"Reuben, why must we live with these people? We are not one of *them*."

"What do you want me to do?" Reuben was exhausted from the endless argument. "Everyone is in the same situation."

"That is not true. Moses Suesser and his family live in a grand flat by themselves. I heard that they even brought their own furniture, not to mention the fact that they have all the food they want."

"Miriam, Suesser owned half of Kraków and had holdings in Warsaw. He sold everything right before the invasion, at a handsome profit I might add, and withdrew all his money from the banks. He predicted the future."

Miriam stared at the bare floor and massaged her temples. "Reuben, my nerves cannot take any more of this."

Jacob had heard enough. "Miriam, I have searched the ghetto, and there is no place reserved for people like you. I wish there were, because if we got rid of you two, the rest of us would have some peace."

"How dare you speak to me that way, Jacob Goldberg? Reuben, do something."

"Jacob"—Reuben wagged his finger—"you have been nothing but crude and insulting. I demand an apology."

Jacob's long-building hatred for the man surfaced. "When are you going to get it through your head that you are no better than anyone else? We all hate living in this filthy, disease-ridden hellhole. My baby died, and I could do nothing. Nothing. Now I am forced to watch my son waste away. If you can find somewhere better, good riddance to you and your wife."

Miriam pushed herself from the floor. "We have had losses, too. Our former lives were filled with friends and parties."

"You think you can compare losing your friends to the loss of a *child*?" Rose shouted.

Jacob caught his wife as she lunged at Miriam.

"No, I did not say that. I only ask that you have empathy for those who, well, those who came from . . . " She searched for the right words. "You must admit that Reuben and I had much more to lose than you and your family."

Rose squirmed in her husband's arms. "You cow!"

"Calm down, Rose. There is no use."

She broke Jacob's hold and held up her fists.

"Stop, Rose! You will hate yourself if you hit that woman."

"I will not hate myself half as much as I hate her."

"Let us go outside for a bit." Jacob took her hand and pulled her out of the flat.

ଓଓଓଓଓଓ

That night, Jacob awoke to loud moaning. Reuben and Miriam had slit their wrists, and he got to them just as the last of their blood dripped onto the filthy mattress beneath them.

"Melek, wake up. Reuben and Miriam slit their wrists. We have to get them out of here before Anshel wakes up."

"Are they dead?"

"Yes."

ଓଓଓଓଓଓ

Jacob was not immune to the diseases that ran unchecked through the ghetto and contracted typhus.

"Before I die, Rose, I want you to know that I am sorry."

"Hush. Save your strength." Rose said as she fluffed his pillows.

"I am ashamed that I cannot protect you and Anshel as a man should."

"You do not know what you are saying, darling. Go back to sleep."

He coughed, then used the back of his hand to wipe the blood from his lips. "Forgive me for leaving you and Anshel, Rose."

"Go to sleep and you will feel better in the morning."

Jacob coughed again and turned away as she covered him with the heavy, blood-stained quilt Reuben and Miriam Gomulka had left behind. He cringed when he felt himself soil the sheets. The flat had not had running water for months, and Rose cleaned him with dry, dirty rags.

A bitter, mean man named Isidor Teitelbaum had replaced Reuben and Miriam. He was an instigator and reveled in his ability to turn people against one another.

"For Christ's sake, Rose," Isidor said. "Get him out of here. I cannot stand that stench."

After her argument with Miriam Gomulka, Rose had promised herself she would not argue with the others. Isidor tested her resolve. "My husband has typhus. I will care for him."

Anshel burst into the flat. "Mama, I went under the wall and got some bread. See, two loaves . . . well, really one and a half. Let me tell you how I did it."

With a child's excitement, he told his mother how he squeezed under a gap in the ghetto wall and walked into a bakery. "And I was not afraid at all. I waited until the last customer left and told the baker I wanted to buy bread. Then that son-of-a-bitch—"

"*Anshel!* We do not say those things."

"I am sorry, Mama. The baker wanted to charge me a lot more money than last week. I tried to cry, because that usually makes grown-ups give me what I want, but it did not work with him."

Rose was impressed with her clever boy.

"He said that if I wanted bread and did not have enough money, I could do something else, and then he gave me such a strange look. I just ran out of there as quick as I could. Guess what happened then?"

"What, darling?"

"I ran straight into a lady who had two loaves of bread. She fell down, and I scooped them right up and came straight home."

"That is an amazing story, Anshel. You should be very proud of yourself." Melek tousled the boy's hair. He had become the boy's surrogate father.

Anshel's excitement vanished. He looked at the floor and shuffled his feet. "I did something bad, Mr. Shamir." He took one and a half loaves of rye bread from under his coat. "We are all supposed to share bread, and I ate a whole bunch. Mama, you can punish me. I understand."

Rose wiped his tears. "No, Anshel, you will not be punished. You did a very good thing. We have bread. That is what matters."

"But Papa and Mr. Shamir always say we have to share the food. And I did not share."

"You are just a little boy, my darling, and you do a very grown up thing when you go under the wall. You deserve the bread."

"Mr. Shamir, *you* can punish me, if you want."

Melek crouched. "Anshel, anyone who has to talk to that son-of-a-bitch baker deserves extra bread."

Anshel smiled.

"Rose, let us go into the hallway to talk."

She followed Melek out of the flat to the end of the hall.

"It is no use feeding Jacob," he said as gently and quietly as he could.

"Jacob is getting better, I know it. Today, he said he was hungry," Rose lied.

"We have to be practical. Think of Anshel, Rose. He is the future."

She was desperate to save the only family she had left and said, "But, Melek, I need my husband and Anshel needs his father. I will give Jacob my share."

"Rose, you must think of yourself. What will happen to Anshel if he has no one? I am sorry to say your Jacob will no longer benefit from food. Forgive me—I simply speak the truth."

She bit her fingernails.

"We must save who we can. It is your Anshel who provides and will have the biggest share."

"How much will Anshel have?"

"He will get the rest of the loaf he already ate."

Rose went to her son and took the full loaf. "I will divide this one among the grown-ups. We want you to eat the rest."

"But, Mama, I do not want anyone to be mad."

"No one is angry. Now, eat."

"What do you mean, no one is *angry*," Isidor said. "I have heard enough from you and your little *family*. The kid eats half a loaf of bread before he tells anybody, and you just pat him on the head?"

Rose politely asked Isidor to mind his business.

"As long as I hear this drivel it *is* my business. If you have enough food to spoil your brat, then give me some. I am as hungry as the rest of you."

"You should die today and burn in hell for all eternity." The venom in Rose's voice startled the man.

◌◌◌◌◌◌

It was a warm morning in the ghetto. The men were marched away to build a runway at the new military airport, and children under ten years old attended class in illegal cellar schools. Even under the threat of death, teachers formed small classes and taught the ghetto children to read and write. Ghetto women were supposed to be at work in the textile factories located within the ghetto, but Rose sat with Jacob. Time stopped when his hand grew cold. In her pocket, she rubbed Mama's ring as she heard Mama whispering in her ear. *Rose, my child, Anshel will be here soon and he must not see his father like this.*

Rose pushed Jacob's body to the floor, but she fell as she tried to drag him to the door. For the first time since he contracted typhus, she really looked at him. His pants were at his knees, wet with diarrhea, and his shirt was unbuttoned. She placed his head in her lap. Mama's ring dug into her thigh from the weight of his head. *Gravity.*

She scooted from beneath her dead husband, and her muscles strained as she pushed and pulled his body the open window. His shoulders got caught on the window sill, and she adjusted his body until they broke free. His head bumped against the brick as he tumbled to the dirt. She closed the window left the apartment She could not bear to look down to the courtyard.

Chapter 20. Only Rumors

The Kraków ghetto was buzzing with activity. The *Judenrat*, a panel of elders from the Jewish community, was meeting with a prisoner who had escaped Auschwitz. They believed cooperation was the only way to keep their German masters from entirely liquidating the ghetto, but he was trying to convince them otherwise.

"Terrible things happen at Auschwitz. Trains full of Jews—cattle cars that have human beings packed in so tightly they cannot sit—arrive two or three times every week. Their journey lasts for days without food or water. At the camp, Jews are selected to work or die by gas—"

"Stop." The Judenrat president pounded his fist on the desk. "I will not allow a tailor from Warsaw to spread rumors in the ghetto. What you say cannot be true. Our current situation is not ideal, but if we cooperate, we will survive."

"Mr. President, with respect, you are all damn fools. Every Jew is being murdered. The ghettos are nothing more than temporary gathering centers before Jews are sent to die. Cooperation means nothing. How do you not see that?"

"Starving women? Gassing children?" The president walked the tailor to the door. "Even if your story is true, there is no point in alarming everyone. It is bad enough without wild rumors."

The tailor broke the president's grip. "Auschwitz is a death factory. When a train arrives, an SS doctor decides, in an instant, if a person lives or dies. The strong live, the old, the sick, and women with children are sent to the gas chambers. Those who live work at hard labor, and if work or guards do not kill them, starvation does. Dead Jews are burned in ovens day and night. You must gather everyone in the ghetto and fight."

"With what? Spoons and bowls? Women and children? We have nothing—no weapons, no money, and no strength. We work with the Germans. We negotiate. After all, we have not done so badly, have we? We are still here. The Germans demand furs, and we give them furs. The Germans demand money, we give them money." He spoke to the tailor as though to a child who had woken from a nightmare. "I see that you are very upset. We will find a nice woman to take care of you. Rest will do you good."

The tailor wore stolen clothing. When he lifted a pants leg, he revealed a blue-and-white-striped uniform. "Prisoners are stripped of everything, and this is what we are left with." He raised his left sleeve, exposing his tattoo, and said, "We become numbers."

"That is enough, little tailor from Warsaw. Get out of here and go back where you came from. You bring nothing but trouble."

"Sir," a boy, no more than ten years old said, knocking, "you must leave now; you cannot be late."

"Oh, yes—I almost forgot. You will say nothing more about this, little tailor. There is to be no panic in the ghetto."

With that, the Judenrat president put his worn coat over his shoulders and placed an oil-stained hat on his head. It took just a few minutes to arrive at SS headquarters, where he was ushered into a bright, cheery office where the ghetto commandant waited for him.

"The ghetto is to be liquidated the day after tomorrow," he said as he sipped his afternoon tea.

"I beg of you, sir, do not liquidate the ghetto. The Jews are skilled laborers, and we will work longer hours, sir."

"I have wasted enough time with the Jews of Kraków." The commandant spoke as he would to a child. "We demanded furs and what did we get? A few rags, nearly worn through. That simply will not do. I am certain you understand the position you Jews have put me in."

Tears rolled down the Judenrat president's face. "But, sir, when you asked for fur, we gave thousands upon thousands of pieces—nothing was hidden. Sir, you must believe me; we turned over every fur in the ghetto."

The commandant was fed up with the man before him who begged for the lives of the filthy vermin in the ghetto. "Shut up. I cannot stand idly by while you people refuse to follow orders. No, Jew, the ghetto is to be liquidated."

"Sir, please . . . "

"Get out, Jew."

Less than an hour had passed when the old man stood before the Judenrat with his hat in hand and his head hung low.

"The ghetto is to be liquidated." He rubbed his forehead to hide his tears. "We will begin organizing the deportation immediately."

"Where are they sending us?" the vice president asked.

"East."

"We must fight."

"Fight? We have no training and no weapons. We can only hope our cooperation is enough to keep some of us alive."

"Are you mad?" the vice president shouted. "The tailor was right; we should have fought when we still could."

The president looked away. "We should have done many things."

1943

Chapter 21. Deportation to Hell

"Rose! Rose!"

Rose leaned out of the window. "What is it, Melek?"

"They have Anshel."

Rose exited the flat and flew down the stairs.

"The Jewish police caught some boys crawling under the wall and called the Germans. They got Anshel. Hurry!"

They ran until Rose saw fifteen children with their arms above their heads, long before she got to the wall. The smuggled food was on the ground, flattened by German boots.

"Jew-bastards, this means death. Death to you all!" an officer shrieked as he shoved his pistol into the boys' faces.

Rose dove for the officer's legs. "Sir, please, my son is just a little boy; he does not know what he is doing. Please, sir!" She kissed the officer's boots. "Sir, my son will never . . . "

The officer's boot connected with her face, and she landed three feet away. Anshel cringed, his dirty face streaked with tears.

She crawled back to the officer and pressed her bloody ear against his leg. "Sir, I have a diamond ring. It is beautiful. You can give it to your girlfriend."

"Where is it?"

Rose frantically searched her pockets. "Sir, I do not have the ring here. Come with me—I know where it is. Please, sir, please. He is just a little boy."

The officer pointed to Anshel. "Is this your son?"

"Yes, sir, but please, he is all I have, sir, please."

She heard the gunshot a split second before Anshel's chest exploded.

"Madam, if you had this imaginary *ring*, your son would still be alive."

"You bastard."

The officer fired his pistol into Melek's forehead. Then he shot each child in the neck and laughed at Rose. "One down. Where is the ring? Another one down. Where is the ring?"

Later, Rose found Mama's ring in the flat, sparkling in the sunlight that streamed through the window she and Jacob had fought so hard for. She had lost Mama, Papa, Tzeitel, Jacob, and Anshel. Mama's ring had lost its meaning. Too tired to die, she fell asleep until she heard screaming and noise from a speaker repeating orders as it rolled through the ghetto.

"Jews. You are being resettled to the East. Gather your things. Twenty kilos for each."

Rose had nothing left to pack and ran to the square by the front gate. The others already in the square were lined up in rows of twenty. She took a place in line.

"Ghetto Jews," the loudspeaker said, "resettlement day has arrived. You will love the East, Jews."

"Hmpf, we are not going '*east*,'" Rose mumbled.

The man on her left whispered, "I heard a tailor escaped from a place where they are killing Jews by the thousands. Take it from me, that is where we are going."

Two thousand Jews, the last in Kraków, marched to the train depot and were stuffed into twenty cattle cars.

The train engineer sat in the cab with his breakfast of two hard boiled eggs, an apple, and coffee his wife had packed for him. He had seen every imaginable cargo during his thirty years with the railroad. The past two or three years, the cargo had been humans. Well, not humans really—Jews. It was all the same to him. The pay was good, he got extra vodka, and he was home every night.

"What is our destination today?" the coalman asked.

"Auschwitz."

"I never heard of it."

The engineer downed the last bit of bitter *Ersatzkaffee*. "Oświęcim, stupid. They changed the name."

"When I was a child, I visited my cousins there during the summer. There wasn't much to do, but it was pretty. I remember the Soła River . . . "

"There will be no time to visit; we drop the load outside town. Here they come. Stay here and keep out of the way."

The cattle car door slid shut, and Rose's eyes adjusted to the darkness. One hundred sweaty, stinking bodies were pressed together so tightly she had to hold her arms straight up to avoid being crushed. Her face was inches from a man whose foul breath made her gag. As she turned her head, she caught a clump of another woman's long, greasy hair in her lips. She spat it out, but the sensation of hair in her mouth remained.

There was not enough space in the cattle car to feel the jerk when it began to roll. Rose closed her eyes, and her body relaxed when she heard Jacob's voice teasing her about her cooking and then felt the worm Anshel had proudly gifted her when he was three years old. Her heart filled with happiness until Tzeitel appeared, lying on a corpse, her little arms stretched out, begging to be cuddled.

Water from a metal bucket the Germans had left near the door sloshed and splashed until it toppled. They had also left an empty bucket, a toilet for the passengers. It was a quarter full when it was inadvertently kicked over, leaving the Jews no choice but to relieve themselves where they stood. Rose waited hours before her bladder bested her modesty.

Putrid air and body heat made the enclosed space unbearable. Those who achieved unconsciousness were admired, and those who died were envied. Rose did her part and helped clumsily maneuver bodies through the car. At first, she briefly mourned each death, but then her mourning turned to secret joy when she had enough room to bend her knees and twist her shoulders.

The cattle car rocked rhythmically and lulled many of the Jews into complete boredom. In other circumstances, they would have filled the hours with lively conversation, but it did not seem right to start a conversation with the back of someone's head or with the face an inch away. Passing corpses from person to person was a welcome break—at least it was something to do.

Two stacks of bodies thinned the crowd enough for Rose to sit on the filthy wooden floor. After standing for hours, it meant nothing when dampness from other peoples' waste soaked through her coat. She kept her hand in her pocket and rubbed Mama's ring, while her mind screamed about the unfairness of a world that took away everyone she loved.

She ignored the sound of tongues smacking dry lips from those who tried to produce saliva in their mouths. Jacob used to tease her by chasing her around, making a similar sound as loudly as he could until she laughed. Her head bobbed, and she snoozed until she felt blood from the inside of her cheeks where they rubbed against her dry teeth.

The surviving Jews fell against each other when the train stopped and complained about the engineer's incompetence. They righted themselves and waited an hour for the cattle car to slide open.

Sunlight hurt Rose's eyes, and she cursed the Germans for leaving them in the darkness for two days. She regained her vision and accepted assistance from a prisoner in a striped uniform with matching hat. His bony hand signaled to her to sit on the edge of the cattle car and jump three feet to the wooden platform. Uniformed men with rifles, some with dogs that barked nonstop, screamed at the new prisoners to leave their things, separate by sex, and get ready to march to camp. Fifty yards from the platform, a frumpy farm wife watched as the Jews vacated the cattle cars. Then, she picked up a clothespin and hung the rest of her laundry to dry in the strange-smelling air.

Chapter 22. New Arrivals

A loudspeaker blared, "Men over the age of fifteen and under the age of forty-five, form a line to the left. All women, children, and the elderly form a line to the right. Quickly." The orders were repeated in German, Polish, and Yiddish as the Jews got off the train. They moved slowly because they had not seen the sun since their journey began and the bright sunlight hurt their eyes.

Soldiers forced couples apart and women clung to their men, begging the guards to let them stay together. Small children wrapped their arms around their mothers' legs, hiding from the soldiers, the dogs, the whips, and the guns. New arrivals who had the courage to ask questions were beaten.

Helga sweated in the hot sun as she sauntered up and down the length of the platform with her rifle slung over her shoulder. She heard a baby cry. "Shut that thing up or I will."

Before the mother could muffle the child, Helga grabbed it by one tiny ankle and slammed the child's head against a corner of the cattle car until the skull split and blood dripped down the hot metal. She discarded the tiny body onto the track and strutted away from the woman writhing in despair.

Helga looked over the new arrivals and became suspicious when she came across an old woman who kept her hands in the pockets of her dirty, heavy woolen coat. "You with the coat. What do you have in your pocket?"

The old woman said nothing.

Helga changed her tone to put the woman at ease. "Whatever you have, grandmother, you can give it to me for safekeeping."

The old woman trembled. "I have nothing, ma'am. My hands are cold."

"But it is so warm today, you do not need the coat. Give it to me, and I will see that it is well taken care of until you need it. You see, we take care of everyone here at Auschwitz."

"I am simply warming my hands."

Helga's faced hardened. "I order you to take your hands out of your pockets. Immediately."

The woman lifted her hands and Helga fished through her coat pockets.

"What have we here? Such beautiful pearls. Thank you, grandmother. In the future, you must be more cooperative. Please go to the truck with the red cross painted on the side at the end of the platform. It will take you to your new home."

"Ma'am, may I go with my wife?" A man said as he slipped his arm through his wife's. "We have been married for more than forty years and do not want to be separated."

"Of course, sir, you may accompany your wife."

The couple held hands as they shuffled to the end of the platform. They were assisted into the tarp-covered truck with a red cross painted on it and were driven with others who could not walk the short distance to the camp, directly to the gas chambers.

Processing arrivals at the platform could last hours, and to pass the time, Helga played tricks on the new prisoners. She pulled her pistol and aimed into the crowd. "Bang! Bang!" she shouted. She laughed as she counted the number of people who fell to ground.

Josef Mengele, an SS doctor who conducted experiments on prisoners, stood before the line of men. He occasionally inquired about profession or age and with a flick of his wrist, sent the man to live or die. Men with interesting physical traits or obvious illness always gave him pause. If the man could be of use in an experiment, Mengele granted life. For hours, his wrist rotated until the last man was sent to die.

The women's column moved more slowly than the men's, because Mengele enjoyed tickling little children and pinching their cheeks. His warm smile and proper manners soothed the women as he joked, laughed, and decided who would live and who would die.

"How many children, mother?"

"I have no children." Rose's eyes welled with tears at the thought of her beautiful Tzeitel's body lying naked, all alone, waiting to be buried, and little Anshel, standing in a line of children, his hands in the air like a common criminal, then shot dead because she did not have Mama's ring in her pocket.

"My dear, I see that you are upset. You have not had children?"

"I had two, sir. They are both dead."

"Such a shame. A beautiful woman like you, now childless. How old are you?"

"Sir, I am twenty-eight years old."

"Please move to the right."

Mengele rubbed his wrist, the pain from rotating his hand left to right for hours nearly unbearable. "Sergeant, that is enough for today."

Two thousand men, women, and children trudged down a gravel path, five hundred yards, to a long, red brick building with an arched entryway in the middle. The neatly spaced signs outside the barbed wire warning them that the fence was electrified were familiar, and the Jews thought nothing of them. Chimneys spewing flames and black smoke were strange, but no one dared to ask their purpose.

ൟൟൟൟ

Mörder, Günther's German shepherd dog, pranced at his side as they marched the prisoners down the gravel path to camp. The dog was trained to leap five feet into the air, knock a prisoner to the ground, and to methodically rip flesh from bone. She would ignore the victim's screams until she heard the command to release her prey, then she sat on her haunches and thumped her tail until she was granted a brief pat on the head—her reward for a job well done.

She strained at her leash and growled at the frightened people until her master gave the order she loved most. "Mörder. *Angriff.*"

The guards lit cigarettes and watched as the frenzied animal ripped flesh and tore muscle from the bones of one terrified woman. They marveled at the dog's control in starting at her feet then working its way up her body. Blood covered muscle and bone flew out of the Jewess's body. She was still by the time Mörder pulled out her throat. The dog trotted back to her master and sat at his side.

Günther's quick pat on the head was all the dog needed.

ൟൟൟൟ

Helga sidled up to Günther. "What took you so long? I missed you."

"You should have seen it, Helga. It was beautiful. Mörder sensed an escape attempt, made the most beautiful leap, and stopped the Jewess."

A new prisoner protested, "That is not true. This guard commanded his dog to attack a defenseless woman."

Helga reached for her whip, and the prisoner stepped back into line.

Mörder lay in the gravel and licked her fur.

Helga patted the dog. "Good girl, Mörder."

"Poor baby," Günther said, bending down. "You have something on your collar. Do not worry, Daddy will give you a bath." He snapped the leash, and Mörder jumped to his side.

Helga formally greeted the new arrivals. "Jew-whores, welcome to Auschwitz. You have been chosen to work, which you shall do. As you are all Jews, you will shower with disinfectant—you will not keep the lice you have brought with you. You will be shaved, tattooed, issued uniforms, and then taken to the prisoner blocks, where you will be fed. Take off your clothes and place them on the hooks."

As she removed her coat, Rose struggled to shove Mama's ring under her tongue.

Men and women guards ogled as married women who had never taken off their clothes in front of anyone, not even their husbands, stood naked before strangers, and teenagers tried to hide their budding bodies with their arms.

"Move Jew-bitches, we are late."

Five men, all in striped uniforms, sat at a long table, each with the tools of his trade—stacks of forms, pens, ink pads, and tattoo needles—laid neatly before him. The women queued up and told the prisoners their names, carefully spelling both first and last, places of birth, parents' names. On the form, their crime was noted in bold letters: "Enemy of the State."

Rose squirmed when the prisoner pulled her left wrist to him and applied the needle, but he did not loosen his grip until he finished the tattoo. In less than a minute, her identity vanished. She was no longer Rose Goldberg from Kraków. She was prisoner number A200489 from hell.

Helga ordered the naked, newly tattooed women to the next stop on their humiliating journey: the barbers. Emotionless men in striped uniforms cut off the women's hair with scissors dulled by use and left gashes where long, beautiful hair had been. Rose's blood-matted hair fell at her feet, but she said nothing for fear that she would lose the only thing she had left from the time before her world went black.

"To the showers for delousing."

Guards laughed and mimicked the women as they winced when the freezing water mixed with disinfectant hit their fresh wounds. Helga alternated the water from freezing cold to scalding hot and watched her fellow guards try to synchronize their exaggerated movements with the women's.

Helga turned off the water and led the soaking women to piles of dresses made from the same stripped cloth the men wore. Scarves that matched the dresses had been laid next to the dresses, and wooden clogs had been thrown into a mound four feet high. She overheard whispering among the prisoners and shrieked, "Eat? Where do you bitches think you are?" She lifted her club and flattened the closest prisoner's nose with a single blow.

Mama's ring flew out of Rose's mouth as the prisoner fell into her. Helga caught the ring in midair, then spat into Rose's ear, "Thank you, Jew. You are too generous."

Chapter 23. First Day in Hell

Rose marched with her fellow prisoners to Auschwitz's women's camp. The coarse cloth of her prison dress rubbed against her skin, which had been softened by the shower. Underclothes were not part of the uniform, and her hairless body itched everywhere. She scratched her arms, legs, and chest, but modesty kept her from touching the most intimate parts of her body.

At Auschwitz, the women's camp was composed of long, red brick buildings with wooden bunks, three tiers tall, inside. Rose choked on the stench of emaciated women who lived too close together and no longer cared about the urine, feces, and death that permeated their lives. She pushed past women who moaned and called out for their mothers and fathers, then stopped in front of a woman who held a dirty foot to her mouth, biting her toenails.

Rose crawled into an open space on the bottom tier of the bunks, relieved to find somewhere less crowded than those above. She felt something sharp and tiny bounce off her leg.

"Hah! The new ones always start at the bottom, but they learn . . . ."

The Germans appointed someone in each block to keep order among the prisoners, called a kapo. Appointments were given to criminals and prostitutes or those observed to be ruthless with other prisoners. Kapos did not discriminate—no one was immune from their cruelty and desire for power.

"You sleep at lights out. Get up." The kapo swung her club against Rose's wooden clogs.

Rose smashed her head on the bunk above her. Blood ran down her face as she stood at attention. She began to speak but stopped when she felt the elbow hit her ribs, a warning from a nearby prisoner to stay quiet.

"Dinner has arrived. Line up."

There was a mad rush to the door, and scuffles broke out. Just outside the door, two women beat each other. Enthusiastic calls of "Fight! Fight! Fight!" egged the women on until the older of the two picked up a loose brick and smashed her opponent's head until the kapo held back her arms and pronounced her adversary dead.

Rose was shocked by the animalistic display and did not move until another prisoner shoved her to a huge cauldron flanked by two healthy-looking women in striped dresses. Dinner was nothing more than a few rotten vegetables and blackened potato peels in lukewarm water. When she held out the metal bowl she had been issued earlier, the prisoner with the ladle pushed aside the vegetables and filled Rose's bowl with dirty warm water.

After dinner, the women were allowed fifteen minutes at the latrine, then lights out.

Hundreds of prisoners clamored up ladders to the top and middle rows of bunks. They were quite practiced with packing five or ten women in a space meant for two, and within a minute or two, they were packed so tightly in each bunk, they had to turn over as one. While not empty, bottom bunks held only two or three women each and Rose soon discovered why it was only the unlucky few who slept near the floor.

The windows in the block were nailed shut and the body heat soon made it unbearable. Each bunk was separated by a brick wall, and Rose's two bunkmates laid against the cool bricks. She had enough room between them to lie on her back, and she stared at the wood slabs a few inches from her face.

She did not sleep long before she felt a stream of something bouncing on her stomach. Urine from prisoners above fell through the wooden slats, followed quickly by the diarrhea that could not be controlled in the women's sleep.

At four o'clock in the morning, the kapo walked past the bunks and used her club against the bricks and the prisoners while she screamed, "Out of bed. Out of bed."

Rose crawled out of the bunk and stood at perfect attention with the others.

"Your breakfast is outside. Anyone who fights will be sent to the gas."

The breakfast soup was identical to that from the night before, but this meal was supplemented with bread. Rose had not eaten in days, but the bread was infested with maggots, and she could not stomach the thought of putting it into her mouth. She set it down, and the woman next to her swiped it and shoved the whole piece into her mouth.

"How long have you been here?" Rose asked as the woman chewed.

"Two years."

"When I got here, everyone was split up. Entire families were sent different ways. What happened to them?"

"Do not ask questions you do not want the answers to."

"What is that building with flames and black smoke rising high above the chimney?"

"I told you. Do not ask questions. It will do you no good."

The woman who had bitten her toenails said, "You are new here, and you do not understand what Auschwitz is yet. But just like all new prisoners, you will learn quickly."

"I do not understand."

"Do you remember when you first got here, and men were separated from the women, old from young, et cetera? Anyone who was not chosen to work is probably already dead. They were sent to the gas."

Rose could not breathe.

"And those flames? Those are the dead being burned. That is what life is in Auschwitz. If you are not chosen for work, you are gassed then burned. But if you are chosen for work, you may also be gassed and burned. That is, if you do not die some other way. There are many opportunities for death here at Auschwitz. Gassing, beating, hanging, starving. You name it, and someone has died that way. The only thing you cannot do at Auschwitz is live. That is a given and you must accept it."

Chapter 24. Weekend Away

Helga jumped out of bed and grabbed a white blouse and blue skirt from her closet, ran into the communal bathroom, and slammed the door. The skirt was uncooperative, and she tugged on the back zipper until it closed, then tucked the blouse into the waistband. As she looked at herself in the full-length mirror, she noticed that her new ring made a slight bulge in the pocket of her too-tight skirt. *What a shame, to hide such a beautiful ring*, she thought. Slipping it on, she exited the bathroom.

Outside, Günther stomped out a cigarette. "What took you so long?"

"Do not be cross, darling." Helga pouted. "I wanted to look especially nice for our holiday. What do you think?"

"You"—Günther spat out a piece of tobacco that was stuck on his tongue—"look fine."

She fluttered her fingers and the diamonds caught the light. "Is it not pretty?"

"Where did you get it?"

"Let us tell the others it is an engagement ring. They will be so envious."

He nuzzled her ear. "Do not tell anyone it is an engagement ring."

"But why, darling? We have been dating for years. We must get married and start a family."

"I do not have enough money to get married, and I definitely do not want to have children."

"We are going to be married anyway, so why not now? I have more than enough money."

"Helga," he said, kissing her neck, "I never said we are going to get married."

"Yes, you did. Last week you said, 'Someday, I would like to be married.'" She shivered with every kiss.

He pushed her away. "I was talking in generalities. I did not say I was going to marry *you*."

"Stop teasing, Günther." She took his hand. "Let us not quarrel—the others are waiting."

Just eighteen miles from Auschwitz was Solahütte, a resort offered by the SS to its officers and enlisted men for rest and relaxation. Surrounded by forest and boasting a clear view of the Soła River, it was a treat to get away from the drudgery of their daily work.

During the brief bus trip to the resort, Helga sat at the window and pretended not to listen to Günther's conversation with his friend Ludwig.

"I could not find one in the last transport that was worth the trouble. Even last year, they would try to fix their hair when they got off the train. Now they do not bother."

"Ludwig, my friend, that is where you and I part ways. I do not care one way or another how they look."

The bus pulled into the resort parking lot, and the passengers fell into line before the welcoming officer. "I am Dr. Mengele. You may know me as the head doctor at camp. Do not let formalities get in the way while we spend the next days together.

"I am afraid I do not recognize everyone, but I am sure we will remedy that quickly." He glanced at his wristwatch. "You have just enough time to put your things in your rooms and freshen up. Luncheon will be served in the dining hall in thirty minutes."

Helga rushed to Mengele's side. "Dr. Mengele, it is an honor to meet you."

"And what is your name?"

"Helga Küster." She was breathless.

Mengele kissed the back of her hand. "It is an honor to meet you, Helga Küster. I shall look forward to dining with you during your stay." He looked at his watch. "It is a pity, but I must leave you now, so I may supervise the luncheon. It was a pleasure meeting you, Miss Küster."

She wobbled as she returned to Günther.

"Stop it, Helga. He was only being polite." Günther motioned to her bags. "Pick those up. We have to hurry."

"Günther, remember when you would carry my bags for me?"

"That was a long time ago. Keep moving."

They carried their bags to the deck, which ran the length of the long building. Loungers with brightly upholstered, thick padding waited for visitors to take in the sun and unwind. Inside the resort, signs on the staircase directed the women to the second floor and the men to the third floor. Before Günther left Helga on the second-floor landing he said, "I will be waiting in the dining hall in thirty minutes."

Helga threw her bag on the bed in her small room. She used the thirty minutes to shower, put on fresh clothes, and go to the dining hall.

"I see you spent the time wisely," Günther said as she approached.

"I want to make a good impression on everyone. Perhaps we will sit close to the doctor during lunch."

"You can dream, Helga."

A long wooden table, decorated with thirty tall flower arrangements spaced exactly three feet apart, was dwarfed by the enormous dining hall. Terribly thin men with closely shaved heads, dressed in crisp white tuxedo jackets and black pants, went over the dining hall to ensure everything was in perfect order. The waiters were prisoners who showered and wore clean clothes. Work at the resort was a coveted position—it was indoors, and opportunities to steal a bit of food existed.

Helga admired the fine china, silver flatware, and crystal glass place settings and felt proud to find that each piece was emblazoned with a swastika. She found her name written in calligraphy on a white tent place card at the far end of the table, and Günther was next to her. At the head of the table was none other than Dr. Josef Mengele.

"Günther, we are next to Dr. Mengele. My dream has come true!" Her excitement turned to nervousness. "What will I say to him? I do not know how to behave around someone like him."

"This is probably a mistake. Someone will catch it and we will be moved. The officers will not even notice you anyway."

Helga felt her cheeks flush. "Günther, I do not know how to act around the officers."

"They do not even notice you."

The remaining guests streamed in, and everyone rose when Mengele entered.

"Please. Sit. We are here to get acquainted. Waiters, you may serve."

White-coated waiters took drink orders, while black-coated busboys filled water glasses.

"Madam, what would you like to drink, madam?"

Helga fidgeted, afraid Mengele would not approve of her choice. She ordered beer and was relieved when he showed no outward reaction.

Mengele ordered the first course. Busboys scurried through the dining hall to set up tray stands. Huge round trays, each holding eight bowls of steaming chicken broth, floated out of the kitchen on practiced arms and were placed where the waiters could easily serve them to the assembled guests. The service was slow and deliberate—spilling broth was a death sentence.

Busboys anticipated the second course and quickly cleared the bowls of broth as the herring floated out of the kitchen.

Helga loved herring and lifted a heaping forkful. Before it reached her mouth, Mengele gently stopped her arm.

"Savor the herring, my dear. It is one of the pleasures of being on holiday." In his best French accent, he said, "The setting and the food are"—he kissed his fingertips—"*magnifique.*"

A plate crashed.

Mengele jumped out of his seat. "You idiot. The rest of you, finish serving. Idiot, get into the pantry." His eyes landed on Günther. "You have the honor of punishing the idiot."

Günther pushed his chair back.

"No, son, it can wait until your stomach is full. Enjoy your meal."

Günther scooted his chair back in and resumed his lunch.

Dessert was sweet French toast with coffee, after which officers, enlisted men, and other guests slowly exited the dining room.

Mengele slapped Günther on the back. "I am going to join the sing-along. You take care of the idiot."

Helga followed Günther to the kitchen. He flung open a door marked "Pantry" and found the prisoner, whose face was white with flour. "You piece of shit!" Günther yelled as he pulled his sidearm from its holster.

With a single shot, the prisoner's head exploded and left an odd pink paste on the walls.

ଔଔଔଔଔଔ

Helga joined the girls sunning themselves on the resort deck facing the river. She plopped down next to Birgit, a communications clerk at camp, and made exaggerated hand movements as she settled into the lounge chair.

"That is a beautiful ring, Helga. Where did you get it?" Birgit asked.

"Günther gave it to me." Helga's smile did not betray her lie.

"Did he ask you to marry him? Tell me! I am dying to know."

"Really, he asked me not to tell anyone."

"Have it your way." Birgit rubbed her arms. "I am so pale. I envy you—your face always has a healthy glow."

Helga shaded her eyes. "The summer breezes and sun can be glorious, but when it rains, Auschwitz turns into a swamp. My boots get so caked with mud, I can hardly walk. And the winter can be so cold, I have to wear two or three sweaters under my coat to keep warm."

"Can anything be done about the awful smell? Some days it is unbearable, and the prisoners always smell like a sewer. Almost every day, a prisoner will collapse and then just lie there, like this." Birgit imitated a corpse with her eyes open and tongue hanging out.

Everyone on the deck showed their appreciation with laughter and applause.

Birgit bowed to her audience. "Thank you, thank you."

Helga steered the conversation back to her ring. "I am not supposed to tell anyone about it. Günther would be so angry."

"Why would he be angry? I cannot imagine that he would give it to you for no reason."

"You know how shy he is."

"Really?" Birgit scratched her forehead. "I never thought he was shy, considering how flirty he is in the office."

Helga shielded her eyes from the sun. "What do you mean?"

"I am certain he does not mean anything by it."

"Now, Birgit, do not say such things." Helga laid back on the lounge chair. "It is as though you were jealous."

"Forget what I said. He is obviously in love with you. The ring must have cost him a fortune."

Chapter 25. *Appell*

It was late November and early-morning roll calls could be unbearable. To ward off the cold, Helga dressed in a heavy woolen coat over her uniform, black leather gloves, fur-lined boots, and a scarf tied around her neck. She studied a form on her clipboard while she waited for the prisoners to line up in front of the block.

"*Appell. Appell.*"

The prisoners, who wore only their lightweight uniform dresses, stood in rows and shivered.

Helga counted the first row. "There are only forty-eight here—two short. There must have been an escape."

"Madam, two prisoners are dead this morning, madam."

As Helga recorded the dead, she saw a prisoner in the third row sway slightly.

"Jew-whore, what is your number?"

"A200489," Rose said.

Helga recognized the prisoner. "You are the Jew who gave me that wonderful diamond ring."

"I gave you nothing," Rose hissed. "You stole it."

Helga kicked Rose to the ground and viciously beat her with a truncheon. "Get . . . up . . . whore . . . or . . . I . . . will . . . Ouch. The Jew broke my finger. Get the block."

The kapo pointed to a prisoner and together they ran to the administrative building, where implements of torture were stored for easy access. The heavy wooden whipping block left a trail as they dragged it through the dirt to the women's camp. Then the kapo scrunched Rose's dress up around her neck, laid her on her stomach, and with thick, blood-stained rope, tied her hands under the block.

Helga thrust her whip handle at the kapo. "Do it, or you will go first."

The kapo's first lash fell on the ground.

Helga snatched the whip. "Imbecile get away. Whore, you will count each lash. Every time you lose count, we will begin again." She threw the whip over her shoulder and flicked her wrist.

"One."

"I do not hear you."

"One. Two. Three. Four," Rose said through clenched teeth, the sweat from her forehead stinging her eyes.

Helga continued with a steady rhythm.

"Five. Six. Seven. Eight. Seven." Rose closed her eyes and saw rows of corpses laid out side by side.

"No. Start again."

Rose kept her eyes closed and felt the lashes just enough to keep counting. She saw Jacob, Anshel, Tzeitel, Mama, and Papa lying together. Suddenly, Jacob sat up and said something, but she could not hear him. *"Three. Four. Eight."*

"Start again." Helga's whip was soaked with blood.

Rose's mind separated from her body, and she did not feel the pain from the lashes when she saw Jacob again. He was waving her away. "Go back, Rose. You have to show those animals that they will never get us all."

Helga screamed, "Why are you not counting? Count."

Rose started counting. When she said "ten," the lashes stopped, and the pain she felt from the gouges that crisscrossed her back turned into a burning desire to survive.

1944

Chapter 26. Gas Chamber

Helga watched as the *Sonderkommando*, Jewish men forced to aid in death's assembly line, wandered through a large undressing room outside the underground gas chamber. The prisoners helped the elderly undress and spoke to the victims in soothing tones. It was no use to cause panic.

A man and his five-year-old daughter from a shtetl outside Warsaw, hung their clothes neatly on hooks and lined up their shoes under the bench. The little girl clutched a dirty, tailless stuffed puppy to her chest.

Her father crouched to her. "Your puppy must wait here because she will be frightened in the shower."

"Mine."

"Please, darling, give Daddy your puppy. I promise she will be safe." He lifted his coat. "See? I will hide her here."

She let go and made sure her father hid the toy deep in his coat sleeve.

He pointed to the number above the hook. "Two-seven-one. That is where your puppy is waiting. Can you remember two-seven-one?"

She nodded.

"Thank you for being a big girl."

A prisoner scanned the undressing room.

"Madam, they are ready, madam."

Helga shouted, "Into the showers."

The girl held up her arms, and her father carried her into the room where there was gleaming white tile and shower heads hanging from what looked like plumbing on the ceiling. She slipped her thumb into her mouth and put her head on his shoulder. When the heavy steel door closed, and the room went black, his heart broke because he was so sorry he had tried to break her of the habit.

Pellets sounded like a hard spring rain as they rushed down metal columns throughout the gas chamber. The victims choked on gas rising from the floor. Men threw themselves against the door, while others confessed past wrongs or professed their love, and families clung to each other, determined to die together. The little girl's thumb slipped from her mouth. Her father dropped her, then punched and scratched his way to the top of the pyramid formed in the middle of the room by victims desperate for air. He slipped on blood that gushed from the vanquished, until he reached the top and scratched the ceiling to the point his fingernails ripped off. When someone's teeth sank into his thigh, he tumbled down the mountain and was trampled by others fighting their way to the top.

The screams stopped, and huge fans kicked on to ventilate the gas chamber. Men of the *Sonderkommando* assessed the tangled mess of blue-tinted flesh, slick with blood—from wounds inflicted by desperation in the victims' final moments—and human waste. Moishe, a teenager whose studies at Jagiellonian University in Kraków were interrupted in December 1939, carried a pitchfork as he carefully scaled the pyramid. He rolled bodies from the top to the floor, where another prisoner pushed them to the walls for yet more prisoners to stack them onto carts and push them above ground to the crematorium. There, gold teeth were ripped from slacked jaws and women's hair was cut off with dull scissors. After the corpses' last possessions were taken, they were arranged on a metal gurney by threes: man, woman, and child. The arrangement burned the man and child with the help of the woman's fat fueling the fire. When the gurney was tipped upward, the heads disappeared into the fire first, and the oven door was closed.

Deep into the pyramid, tightly entangled bodies had to be separated. Moishe plunged the sharp tines beneath a ribcage and tugged. Someone handed him a shovel, the kind that might be used to clear snow. He raised the handle over his head and hacked off the corpse's arm, then dropped the shovel within easy reach. With the body freed, he lifted it with the pitchfork and rolled it to the floor. He repeated the process every time a body would not budge. In the end, limbs separated from torsos were intermingled with intact corpses.

ଓଓଓଓଓଓଓ

Moishe was forced to prepare a deep pit, to burn bodies in after the ovens had broken down from overuse. He used railroad ties to create a huge grill at the bottom of the pit and soaked the wood with petrol. After a guard lit the wood, prisoners pushed wheelbarrows filled with corpses and dumped them close to the pit. Moishe felt nothing as he dragged, pushed, and kicked bodies into the flames.

Helga snuck up behind Günther and playfully bumped into him. "What are you doing out here? I heard the ovens were repaired."

"They were, but they cannot keep up." Günther flicked a cigarette butt into the pyre. "For a year, we have asked for more ovens, but the

Commandant said, 'ovens are not in the budget.' Can you imagine? They have money for big parties but will not buy more ovens. Morons."

She saw something move in the flames. "What was that?"

"That happens sometimes. If there is air in the lungs, the heat makes the body dance."

"It looks like that one has an erection."

"Helga, grow up. You've seen that before."

"Yes, but never one like that."

Günther yelled out, "Throw another one in. My girlfriend likes to watch."

Moishe leaped into the pit.

"Dammit," Günther said. "Now I have even more paperwork."

Chapter 27. *Kanada*

Most of the prisoners were assigned to heavy work outside the camp, but in fall 1944, Rose was transferred to the coveted *Kanada* commando, where she worked with several other women outside one of the thirty long wooden huts built to store the booty stolen from victims upon their arrival to camp. Rose's commando was assigned to the jewelry hut, but there were others dedicated to clothes or shoes or toys or any of the other items left on the platform at Auschwitz.

Jewelers who had been saved from heavy work or the gas chambers, sat inside the jewelry hut, behind wooden, velvet-covered tables. They expertly tossed costume jewelry into a bucket set on the table and genuine jewelry into another. Outside, as the women sorted the jewelry, they dropped it into sealed boxes and carried the boxes inside for the jewelers.

Outside, Rose noticed an open pack of cigarettes mixed in with the jewelry. "Do you see any guards?" she said to a prisoner sorting jewelry nearby.

The prisoner glanced around. "No. Hurry up."

Rose stooped and secreted the cigarettes into her dress pocket.

"You," Helga pointed at Rose.

Terror blinded Rose as she snapped to attention. If she were caught stealing, she would be sent to the gas chambers.

"Come with me."

Rose's legs refused to move until she saw Helga enter the hut.

"Jew," Helga said to a small man, "what is this worth?" She rained dozens of bracelets, necklaces, rings, and watches onto the black velvet table before an appraiser. Dust on the floor was kicked up by the pieces that bounced off the table. Rose fell to her knees and returned the errant jewelry to the pile above.

With a discerning eye, the appraiser held up a gold-plated chain with small red glass rubies separated by tiny imitation pearls. "Madam, I am sorry to report this is a piece of costume jewelry, madam."

Helga drew her pistol.

He inspected the chain more closely. "Madam, my error. This necklace is made of twenty-four karat gold, genuine rubies and pearls, madam."

"Now this." She held up a ring. "Do not make the same mistake or you will go to the gas."

Mama's ring, Rose thought. *It's still here.* Helga did not notice when Rose doubled over and dry heaved.

"Madam, this ring is exquisite." His admiration nearly exposed his earlier lie. "The large diamond is nearly flawless, as are the smaller two. The band shows wear, but some polish will make it shine, madam."

"What is that?"

"Madam, I do not see anything, madam."

"Idiot, look right there." Her stubby finger pointed to the symbol engraved inside the ring's band.

"Madam, that is the Hebrew symbol for life, madam."

"Hurry up with the rest. I have things to do."

Rose shook with rage.

෬෬෬෬෬෬෬

It was early evening and Rose paced between the red brick women's blocks. She had fifteen cigarettes in her pocket and estimated that the dry, stale tobacco was enough for a potato and maybe a bit of bread. Just as the guards began to shout orders to gather for roll call, Rose noticed Shayna, a prisoner who worked in the men's guards block, hurrying toward the front of camp, hiding something beneath her coat.

Shayna was barely sixteen years old when she had arrived at Auschwitz from Kaunas, Lithuania. Her mother had protected her in the ghetto, dressing her like a boy to keep her from attracting attention. On the platform, a guard had taken notice of the teenager he thought was a boy and took him to cook and clean for the guards.

At the guard's block, he had been surprised to find a well-developed young woman. His disappointment had not stopped him from raping Shayna, and when he was done, he had ordered her to clean her blood off the floor. She had not known it at the time, but she had just been assigned one of the best jobs for a prisoner at Auschwitz—working as maid and housekeeper for the guards. She cooked and cleaned during the day and at night was raped by the guards. Still, she ate leftovers from the meals she cooked, bathed regularly, and kept her hair. She also stole food to barter with the less fortunate.

Rose called out, "Shayna! Come here."

"What do *you* want?"

"I have cigarettes."

Shayna walked across the wide thoroughfare that separated the men's and women's camps and opened her coat. "I have meat, a potato and some bread. What would you like?"

"I will give you five cigarettes for the meat."

Shayna raised an eyebrow. "Are you stealing business from me?"

"I refuse to sleep with pigs."

"Do not be stupid." Shayna posed like a model. "Look at me—my clothes are clean, and I have warm stockings. You can starve if you like. The potato and meat are ten, and I will throw in the bread for an extra five."

Rose could not afford to pay fifteen cigarettes for food. It was late summer, and she needed stockings or a pair of gloves before the weather turned cold. "No. I will give you ten cigarettes for everything."

Shayna snatched all fifteen cigarettes, dropped the food, and ran.

Another prisoner dived for the food. Rose jumped on her back and they rolled in the dirt. A circle of prisoners and guards appeared and shouts of "Fight! Fight! Fight!" ricocheted off the buildings. The bout ended when Rose broke her opponent's nose. Then she stood up, stared straight into the crowd, and swallowed the meat whole.

1945

Chapter 28. Evacuation

In January 1945, the Reich was disintegrating. Still, the German people blindly believed propaganda that hailed imagined military successes, despite constant Allied bombing from the West and Russian superiority in the East.

The sounds of battle had reached the camp, and Auschwitz descended into chaos. An announcement from the camp commandant ordered the guards to gather in the camp commissary.

Helga caught up to Günther as he ran out of the camp.

"Let go of me, Helga. It is over."

"No, Günther, what about us?"

He pried her fingers from his arm. "I said, let go of me."

"You cannot go," she begged. "Nothing is over. The Führer—"

"Helga, you are a fool if you think Germany will win the war. We can *hear*, *see*, and *smell* the Russians. You can stay, but I am getting out of here."

She suddenly saw Günther for what he was—a disloyal coward. "Anyone who says the Fatherland cannot win the war will be executed for treason. The Führer has secret weapons and is in secret peace talks with the Russians."

"Listen, you stupid, stupid, woman. There are no secret weapons or secret talks. Germany is no more. We must flee to the West. The Russians will massacre us. We have a chance to survive with the Americans."

As Günther started to run, Helga called out, "Run back to your mother, little boy."

The camp commandant repeated his order over the loudspeakers, and Helga went to the commissary to join the rest of the guards who had refused to abandon the Führer.

"You are all loyal soldiers, and the Führer will present each of you with the highest honor—the Iron Cross. For now, we must go west and allow our valiant soldiers to defeat the Russians." The commandant drew three circles on a large map of Germany he had tacked onto the wall. "You will transport the prisoners to one of these camps: Buchenwald, Ravensbrück, or Flossenbürg. Each one is approximately four hundred miles away. Split the prisoners into three groups of twenty thousand, with three hundred guards each. Gather guns and ammunition, blankets, and food for yourselves. There will be no time for meals—the prisoners will eat whatever they can find. We must reach the new camps quickly. Before you leave, shoot prisoners in the hospital, as well as those who cannot walk. Complete *Appell* quickly. Küster is in charge. Dismissed."

Helga raced to her room and lifted the false bottom on the trunk she had brought to Auschwitz. One hundred fifty-three pouches of gold were lined up in perfectly straight rows. She threw the pouches into her bag. *I will never have to work again*, she thought. The bag was too heavy, and she threw half of the pouches onto the bed. Then she filled her pockets with jewelry until flashes from diamonds and gold peeked out from under the flaps.

A few hours later, she stood before the guards who would march prisoners to the camps deep within Germany's border. The long wool coat, stretched over five sweaters and three pairs of trousers, made her itch with sweat. "The vehicles with maps and supplies are ready. Lotti, go to Ravensbrück. Otto, to Buchenwald. And I go to Flossenbürg. We must leave immediately!"

On the command to march, more than an hour had elapsed before all the prisoners who were strong enough to walk passed through the camp gate.

Helga drove a truck filled with food for the guards, up and down the column of prisoners on their way to Flossenbürg. She gunned the engine and pretended to speed into the column to close gaps between rows. She shot prisoners who did not catch up and left them in the muddy snow. After marching for several hours, the Wodzislaw train station appeared. Three train engines attached to coal cars waited, the engineers smoking cigarettes and cursing the cold.

In double-time, the prisoners climbed into the coal cars. Muffled screams, coming from the bottom of the car as prisoners were crushed, could not be heard over the shots into the heads of those too weak to climb. Helga signaled to the engineers to depart when the last of the prisoners disappeared into the coal cars or were lying dead by the tracks.

She stopped the train at the Polish border and ordered the prisoners to toss out corpses. Within minutes, coal-darkened corpses covered the ground. Helga kicked the bodies as she walked the length of the train, to make sure none were alive. No one would escape on her watch.

Chapter 29. What the Hell Is That?

In April 1945, an American battalion had set up headquarters near a small German town close to the Czech border. There had been a few skirmishes with German soldiers, and the American battalion commander had ordered a reconnaissance squad into the forest to seek out the enemy.

The squad had not found any enemy positions in hours and had stopped to rest.

"What the hell is that smell, Lieutenant?"

"I don't know, Corporal." The lieutenant put a finger to his lips. "Quiet, boys, don't alert the Krauts."

"My God, I think it is another one." The corporal said, much too loudly.

"Quiet. Another one what, Corporal?"

"I have a buddy who knows a guy in the Eighty-ninth. A couple of weeks ago, the Eighty-ninth found a camp near Gotha full of half-dead prisoners. The guy said the prisoners were walking around like they were in a trance. From what I heard, it had a terrible smell. I imagine it smelled just like this. I thought the guy was exaggerating. Then I figured even if the guy was on the level, there couldn't be another place as bad as he said. I think he said the camp was called 'Buchenwald' or something like that. I think this is the same thing that guy saw—that's a concentration camp, Lieutenant."

"Shit, there's probably gonna be more," the sergeant whispered.

"You two might be right. Whatever is down there, it isn't going to be good."

The lieutenant held up his binoculars. "I see a bunch of people walking around. It looks like they're all wearing striped clothes. Come with me, Corporal. We're gonna go have a look-see. The rest of you, stay here."

The men left behind took cover and readied their rifles.

A twenty-year-old private leaned against a tree and pinched his nose. "I smelled somethin' like this once back home. A storm kicked up, and three days after it was over, me and my daddy went to the neighbor's farm. All the cattle were just layin' there—dead. I'll tell ya, the smell was just awful. I never smelled anything as bad as that, until now. Well, look at that, boys." He pointed to the white sheets fluttering against the guard tower nearest the gate. "The Krauts just surrendered."

The lieutenant and corporal were cautious as they crossed the road. When they reached the gate, the stench was overwhelming, and the corporal vomited.

"Get up, Corporal. The Krauts just surrendered."

The corporal ran the back of his hand over his mouth. "Looks like it's over for these guys, huh, Lieutenant?"

"Yep. This is the easiest bunch of Krauts I've ever taken. Go back to the squad and—"

"Holy shit." The corporal pointed to corpses piled neatly to the roofs of almost all the wooden barracks and vomited again.

"This is bad. I have to radio HQ." The lieutenant turned back and signaled to the men waiting in the forest to join him. The shocked men stopped cold at the sight and smell of the camp.

"What are we gonna do with all these people?"

"That is for the captain to decide. Sergeant give me the walkie-talkie."

The sergeant did not hear the order through his shock.

"Sergeant"—the lieutenant shook the radioman's arm—"get the captain on the line. He has to know about this."

"Easy-Love-Able, this is King-Sugar-Able, do you read? Over."

"This is Easy-Love-Able. Go ahead, King-Sugar-Able. Over."

"Here you go, sir."

The lieutenant put the walkie-talkie to his ear. "This is Lieutenant Gastaldi. We found another camp. Over."

"Repeat. Over."

"We found some kind of a camp. It looks like the prisoners are civilians. Over."

"What is your position. Over."

"We are on the east side of the forest, by the road to Flossenbürg. You can't miss us. Over."

"King-Sugar-Able, hold your position. Out."

The soldiers waited for the captain to arrive. Prisoners pushed their hands through the barbed wire and begged for food. The Americans did not understand their words, but knew what the filthy, stinking captives wanted.

"Stay alert, men. There are still some Krauts here, and we don't know what they are up to."

A German soldier climbed down a guard tower ladder and was attacked by prisoners. They tore at the man's clothing and beat him bloody.

"Sir, should we stop them? They are gonna kill that guy."

"Nope. Until we get into the camp, that is none of our business."

"What about the rest of the Krauts?"

"They'll stay put. I don't think they are stupid enough to come down. Here's the captain now."

When the Jeep stopped, the captain's face was pure white.

"Captain? Captain?"

"Lieutenant, what the hell is this?"

"It's a concentration camp, sir. I don't know how many prisoners are in there."

"Any Krauts?"

"Yes, sir. There seem to be a few in the guard towers. One of 'em got out, but the prisoners tore him to shreds. I don't think we will see the rest for a while."

"Open the gate. I'm going in. Have the radioman call up HQ for men and supplies, especially food. We're going to help these people." He put his handkerchief to his nose and held himself in check as he gently pushed through the crowd of prisoners. *Son of a bitch*, he thought, *I was on Omaha, got through the Bulge, I've even killed men in hand-to-hand combat, but this . . . this is . . . indescribable.*

"Captain, I think you should make an announcement. You know, make it official?"

"Not until we get the Krauts out of here. I want those bastards alive."

"Yes, Captain."

The lieutenant gathered his men and walked the perimeter of the camp. At every guard tower, Germans surrendered. A total of nineteen guards backed down ladders and went from members of the master race to prisoners of war.

"The POWs are outside the camp, sir. What should we do with them?"

"Thank you, Lieutenant. Just have a couple of men watch them. Tell them they can shoot if the Krauts try to escape. But they don't shoot unless there is a real attempted escape. I don't want to have to explain to HQ why a whole bunch of Krauts were shot in the back. Understand?"

"Understood. Captain, you should make an announcement to the rest of the camp. I can take you to the PA."

In a dark office, filing cabinet drawers were open, and papers were strewn everywhere. The Germans had tried to destroy evidence of their crimes but did not have time to finish the job. The captain switched the PA system on and held the microphone to his mouth. He spoke slowly. "This is

Captain Abram of the 359th Infantry Regiment of the Ninetieth US Infantry
Division. You are free."

The lieutenant looked out the window. "I don't think they understand,
sir."

Abram searched his memory for his grandmother's Yiddish. This was
the first time he would use it since she died. "*Ir . . . zent . . . um, bafreyt.*"

Shouts of thanks to the Americans and God erupted, and those prisoners
who still had some strength danced. What seemed like an unending mass of
men in striped uniforms swarmed out of the wooden barracks. The
Americans suddenly understood languages they had never even heard of
minutes earlier. Joy, relief, and hunger need no translation.

Outside the camp gate, Captain Abram looked over the POWs. *Killing
one of them might be worth a court martial.*

"Sir," the corporal said as he saluted, "we have relieved them of their
weapons. One of them speaks some English."

"Thank you, Corporal. Did he say anything useful?"

"The only thing he said is, 'we were just following orders.' I think he's
full of shit. Pardon my French, Captain."

"I agree with you, son. Take the POWs where the prisoners can't see
them. If they ask for anything, the answer is 'no.' I don't give a damn if
they shit all over themselves or call for their mothers. They don't get a thing
until HQ decides what to do with them."

The corporal hurried back to the POWs. A German smiled at him, and
the corporal pointed his rifle at the man's nose. "Kraut bastard."

"*Nein, nein.* No Nazi. No Nazi."

"You are just Goddamn lucky there are other people around. Because if
there weren't, I swear I would blow your fucking head off."

The soldier pointed to himself. "Friend. I am friend."

"Oh, so now you are my friend? What makes you think that I need a Nazi
friend?"

"*Nein* Nazi." He extended his arm as though to shake hands. "*Kumpel.*
Pal."

"You sure as hell ain't my pal." The corporal pushed the arm away with
his rifle. "You like killin' people, don't you? Well, *heinie*, do you just like
killin' people?" Spittle landed in the POW's eyes.

"Corporal. Enough."

"Aw, we're just getting to know each other, Captain."

"Don't get too chummy."

Chapter 30. Give It Back

Rose peeked out of the block door. She and the other prisoners heard the American's announcement, but there was no guarantee that it was not the Germans using another way to torture them. A smile crept across her face when she saw the guard she hated more than any other, running toward her screaming, "You Jew-bitches will never get out of here alive!"

The women poured out of the block and surrounded the red-faced guard.

Helga lifted her pistol. "I am warning you, get back into the block, or you will be severely punished."

The women continued to surround her.

"Listen to me. The Americans do not care about you. When they see what we have done, they will thank us."

The women moved closer.

"Get back or I will shoot."

"You will not shoot, bitch, while the Americans are here," Rose said.

"That does not matter, Jew-whore," Helga hissed. "Get back or I will shoot."

The women moved closer and closer until Helga could not stretch out her arms.

"I swear that I was only following orders. It was never personal. I had no choice. You must believe me."

Rose grinned at the guard's pleas. "Do you think that if you beg we will leave you be?"

Mortified, Helga dropped her pistol, unbuckled her holster, and threw it onto the dirt. "I am unarmed," she said, her voice quivering.

"We were always unarmed."

Helga emptied her pockets of the currency, jewelry, and pouches of gold she carried with her and opened one of the bulging pouches. "It is full of gold. And here." She pulled a wad of currency from a pocket inside her jacket. "American money." She fanned the one-hundred-dollar bills. "There are thousands of dollars here; you will be able to live like a queen with this money."

"I do not care about your money. Give it to me or I will kill you." Rose could not think of anything she wanted more than to see the Nazi bitch die a slow, painful death.

"I do not know what you want."

"You know what I want, bitch."

"Here. Take everything. It is all yours." Tears and snot dripped down Helga's face as she showed the women her empty pockets. "That is all I have. I swear it."

Rose worked through knots of tangled necklaces, bracelets, earrings, rings—everything Helga had stolen from her people. Suddenly, Mama's ring bounced off Helga's shoe. Rose's deep sadness for all that was lost overwhelmed her as she sucked dirt off the ring and held it up to the sunshine. She thought of Mama, Papa, Jacob, Anshel, and Tzeitel, and the revenge she had plotted since Helga stole Mama's ring. "Mama, I swear, no matter what, I will keep this ring safe forever."

"You found what you wanted? Good, I hoped that you would."

With Mama's ring in her hands, Rose backed out of the circle. "She is all yours, ladies."

Chapter 31. Runaway

An ex-prisoner was felled by a gunshot, and the women left Helga to find the murderer. When the offending guard saw the horde coming toward her, she ran backward and yelled, *"Tue mich bitte nicht weh. Tue mich bitte nicht weh."*

In the moment before she was surrounded, she caught the eye of an American lieutenant who was investigating the gunshot. "American. *Hilf mir, bitte.*"

The soldier understood German and simply watched until she was hidden by striped dresses, then shouldered his weapon, did a crisp about-face, sauntered down the gravel path to the front gate, and left her to be drawn and quartered by the women she had so thoroughly tortured.

As the women attacked the guard, Helga slipped unseen into the block where clothes from the last shipment of Jews were stored. Many of the clothes were too small, owing to the former owners' efforts to take in blouses and skirts here and there to accommodate their shrinking bodies as they starved in ghettos or in hiding.

She unbuttoned her coat and blouse with one hand and shook them off as she rifled through the clothes. With no time to find the perfect fit, she chose a red dress and slipped it over her head. After she stepped out of her uniform skirt, the dress hung to her ankles. She ripped off the yellow star expertly sewn over the heart and cursed its six-pointed shadow. A red and black houndstooth-patterned coat hid the evidence of the dress's origin.

A pair of worn-out shoes would complete the ensemble, but she did not have time to search through the scattered, unmatched men's and women's shoes, many stuffed with newspaper or straw in attempts to stop rain, sleet, and snow. Her own highly polished boots could give her away, so she rubbed dirt into the leather.

Her survival depended on blending in with the townspeople of Flossenbürg. She carefully opened the block door. The forest was only one hundred yards from the back gate, but she would have to climb through a deep ditch inside the perimeter of the camp that had been built to deter prisoners from throwing themselves against the electrified fence.

When she was convinced the coast was clear, she sprinted toward the ditch. Her jump fell short and slimy mud clung to her hair, oozing through her clothes and into her shoes. She fought the mud for several long minutes, until she was out of the ditch. Unsure of herself and her new appearance, she slipped out an open gate and made her way through the forest.

Helga rinsed herself off in a stream. She was still wet when she reached the town square. American soldiers with their rifles lazily slung over their shoulders were surrounded by children with traces of Hershey bars melting on their lips and chins. They excitedly jabbered at the men who seemed to have an unlimited supply of the sweet chocolate many children had never tasted.

She skirted the square and joined a crowd of townspeople cursing their fate as they watched the Americans. A man with a kind face noticed Helga.

"What happened to you?" he asked.

"Sir," she whispered, "can you help me?"

"What do you need?"

"I must hide."

He put a fatherly arm around her shoulders. "Come with me."

They wandered through the crowd and down a side street until they were stopped by a soldier. Helga pretended to cry and told the American she just learned her husband was missing in action in the East. The soldier thought of his girlfriend back home and sent the pair on their way.

PART III. JUSTICE?

1964

Chapter 32. Decision

John Christensen, the prosecutor at Helga's deportation hearing, was exhausted from telling the difficult story of Rose and Helga. "That is all I have, Your Honor."

"Thank you, Mr. Christensen." The judge turned to Helga's defense attorney. "Mr. Huber, would you like to begin your defense today, or do you prefer to start fresh in the morning?"

"If it pleases the court, I would like to begin today."

"Mr. Huber, please keep aware of the time. We will break at exactly four o'clock."

Ed Huber straightened his papers on the defense table, then rose to address the court. "Your Honor, it is inconceivable that my client, Mrs. Helga Roth, is guilty of any crime, much less the crimes the prosecution alleges. She has been a law-abiding citizen of the United States since 1947, and it is not logical that, if Mrs. Roth committed these alleged crimes in her native Germany, she would control herself for this length of time in her adopted country. My client has spent the last seventeen years as a law-abiding citizen of the United States.

"I submit, Your Honor, that my client is incapable of the alleged crimes *and* is innocent of lying on her immigration application. I will prove that during World War Two, Mrs. Roth worked in a defense plant, just as American women worked in defense plants during the war. In addition, I intend to prove that, like American women, Mrs. Roth prayed for her country's victory—a demonstration of patriotism, not an indication she committed violent acts against others."

Rose bit the inside of her cheek. *I wonder how many American women tortured Jews during the war.*

"I do not know how much more of this I can listen to, Rose," Samuel whispered.

"Shush, Samuel."

"Your Honor, I am afraid that we have strayed from the reason that we are here, and that is to determine whether Mrs. Roth was or was not truthful on her application to immigrate to the United States. While the prosecution's opening statement was compelling, it did not address the main issue.

"I would like to point out that the application itself is flawed regarding an applicant's past affiliations. The language may be intimidating to those who do not possess a full understanding of the intricacies of United States law. For instance—"

"I am aware of the application's shortcomings, Mr. Huber."

"Ultimately, Your Honor, it is up to you to help the prosecution understand that my client, Mrs. Helga Roth, did nothing wrong with her application to immigrate to the United States, unless the humanness of being intimidated by unfamiliar circumstances is a criminal act. I have nothing further, Your Honor. Thank you."

"Court is adjourned."

At precisely nine o'clock the next morning, Christensen called Rose to the stand and waited for her to make herself comfortable in the witness box. He and Rose had gone over his questions many times in preparation for her testimony.

"Mrs. Berzon, the court is sympathetic to how difficult it was for you to come forward when you discovered Mrs. Roth was living in the United States. I have just a few questions. How do you know the defendant?"

"She was a guard in the women's camp at Auschwitz." Rose held Christensen's eyes.

"What was your position at the camp, Mrs. Berzon?"

"I was a prisoner."

Helga scribbled something on a yellow legal pad and nudged her attorney. He read the note and shook his head.

"Did my opening statement reflect the facts of your life accurately?"

"Yes, Mr. Christensen. You were very thorough."

"Did I exaggerate in any way?"

"No, sir, you did not."

"Were my statements regarding Mrs. Roth's actions at Auschwitz concentration camp accurate, Mrs. Berzon?"

Rose looked at Helga.

"I can only say that the facts concerning my encounters with Mrs. Roth were accurate."

"Those are all the questions I have for you, Mrs. Berzon. Thank you."

Huber approached the witness box and was careful not to appear confrontational with Rose. "Mrs. Berzon, thank you for agreeing to speak with the court today. I am afraid I have more questions than Mr. Christensen. Would you like a glass of water before we begin?"

Rose promised herself she would stay strong. "No, thank you, Mr. Huber."

"Mrs. Berzon, it has been almost twenty years since you say that you saw Helga Küster when you were both in Poland. Why do you believe that Mrs. Roth is the guard you encountered at Auschwitz?"

"Mr. Huber, when she was a guard at Auschwitz, her shrill voice followed me. I still hear it every day. There is no mistaking it; the voice I heard at the grocery store belonged to Helga Küster." She reached for a tissue and dabbed her eyes.

Huber had planned to press Rose on how she had identified Helga but thought it better if he did not make the small woman, a former prisoner in a concentration camp, cry. He moved ahead with the next line of questioning. "Was Helga Küster the only guard at Auschwitz?"

"There were many guards at Auschwitz."

"Mrs. Berzon, forgive me. As there were many guards, how can you be sure Mrs. Roth is the Helga Küster you knew as a guard at Auschwitz?"

"Mr. Huber, I remember very clearly the woman who stole my mother's ring from me." Mama's ring felt heavy on Rose's hand.

"The prosecution said a guard took your ring during processing. Do you agree with that statement?"

"I agree with Mr. Christensen's statements, Mr. Huber. He was truthful."

"Was Helga Küster the only guard who supervised the processing of prisoners at Auschwitz?"

"No, many guards processed prisoners."

"Again, I ask you, Mrs. Berzon, how can you be sure that my client, Mrs. Roth, was the same guard who took your mother's ring?"

"Mr. Huber," Rose said, wiping her eyes, "I can never forget the beast who ripped the last piece of my family from me."

"That is all the questions I have. Thank you, Mrs. Berzon."

Rose stepped down from the witness stand and sat next to Samuel. His touch calmed her heart.

Huber had prepared Helga to take the stand, but just as he was to call her, she grabbed his arm and said, "I will not be questioned."

"Your Honor, may we have a ten-minute recess?"

"Ten minutes, Mr. Huber."

Helga followed Huber into a small room adjacent to the courtroom.

"Mrs. Roth, you must take the stand."

"It is not necessary, Mr. Huber. The judge did not believe one word the Jew or that Jew-loving attorney said."

The court reconvened, and the spectators gasped when Huber announced that his client did not wish to take the stand.

"Quiet in the courtroom. Mr. Huber, does your client understand that it is her right to take the stand to answer these charges?"

"Yes, Your Honor. I have fully explained her right to defend herself on the stand."

"Mrs. Roth, is it your decision that you are waiving your right to take the stand in your own defense?"

Helga's chair scraped on the floor. "Yes."

"Very well. Mr. Christensen, you may begin your closing statement."

Christensen paced the length of the courtroom. "Your Honor, we have heard from Mrs. Berzon, the victim of Mrs. Roth's actions in the horrifying place known as Auschwitz concentration camp, and with Mrs. Roth's near-admission of her Nazi Party affiliation during her INS interrogation, the only conclusion that can be drawn is that by omitting these facts from her immigration application, Mrs. Roth violated the laws of the United States. It is your duty, Your Honor, to send Mrs. Roth back to her native country and send a message to others who lied to enter the United States: they will not be allowed to continue to live as their victims' neighbors.

"That is all I have, Your Honor. The prosecution rests."

"Court will adjourn for lunch."

଼ଔଔଔଔଔଔ

At exactly one o'clock, the judge asked Huber to begin the defense's closing argument.

"Your Honor, while Mr. Christensen has described terrible crimes the world should never see again, your task is not to judge the crimes of Nazi Germany, but to judge the merits of the claim that Mrs. Roth made false statements on her immigration application. Your Honor, as you are aware of the difficulties with the questions on the immigration application, I believe that you will find that Mrs. Roth did, in fact, answer the questions to the best of her ability, and she should not be penalized for bureaucratic mistakes completely out of her control. The defense rests. Thank you, Your Honor."

"Thank you, Mr. Huber and Mr. Christensen. I will present my findings in ten days. Court adjourned."

For nine days, Rose cleaned and cooked elaborate dinners to keep from thinking. On the tenth day, she awoke, dressed slowly, and walked to the car, her arm linked with Samuel's, dreading the ride to the Loop.

Once in the courtroom, Rose and Samuel sat in the front row, behind Christensen, as they had every day during the hearing. She felt the same terrible dread she had more than twenty years earlier, when she had first encountered that beast. A heavy wooden door squeaked open, and Helga followed her attorney to the defense table. The chill that went through Rose made her entire body numb. She lost her breath when the judge entered carrying the manila folder that held Helga's future.

Judge Bodden took his place behind the raised bench and was deliberate in his movements as he removed a single sheet of paper from his folder. He took a deep breath before he spoke. "Ladies and gentlemen, I have been asked to assess Helga Roth's honesty in answering questions on her immigration application. After hearing the facts presented and with careful consideration, I find Mrs. Helga Küster Roth falsified her immigration application to ensure her admittance to the United States and order her deported to her native Germany immediately. Mrs. Roth will remain in custody until deportation is arranged. Court is adjourned."

Rose did not move until the heavy wooden door shut Helga out of her life forever.

1985

Chapter 33. Last Interview

In 1985, a Nazi hunter from the Simon Wiesenthal Center forwarded a tip to the police department in Nuremberg, Germany, regarding an alleged Nazi perpetrator. The police chief dropped the file onto Sergeant Wannamaker's desk. "Wiesenthal is at it again."

Vincent Wannamaker had been promoted to detective the year before and was assigned the cases no one wanted. He picked up the file and sighed. "Chief, I would rather not do another one of these."

"Those people from the Wiesenthal Center will not rest until they find every single one of their 'criminals.' Get on it today, Wannamaker. I do not want to explain to the mayor or worse, the press, why we ignored the complaint."

Wannamaker packed his briefcase with the suspect's file, a cassette tape recorder, microphone, and ten cassettes, then drove to Helga's last known address.

Inside a nondescript apartment building, he climbed to the fourth floor and found apartment 4D. He double-checked the apartment number, then knocked. A heavyset woman with graying hair opened the door. "Are you Helga Küster Roth?" Wannamaker asked.

"Yes. Who are you?"

"Mrs. Roth, I am Detective Vincent Wannamaker with the Nuremberg Police Department. May I come in?"

"What do you want, Mr. Wannamaker?"

"I have a few questions about a complaint from the Wiesenthal Center. It should take no more than an hour."

When the United States had deported her back to Germany, Helga had realized the unspoken pact among the German people to leave the past behind them had saved her from arrest. She made a comfortable life for herself in Nuremberg and lived in a flat near the home where she grew up. The visit from a detective twenty years later was a shock. "What do they want from me? I have done nothing wrong."

"We should talk about this inside. May I come in?"

She offered the young man a chair at her dining table and sat across from him.

As he set up the tape recorder and microphone he explained the Wiesenthal Center and why the complaint was filed. "When they inform us of someone they suspect is a Nazi criminal, we are obligated to conduct an interview. Do not be concerned, Mrs. Roth. Usually nothing comes of it. Shall we begin?"

"Mr. Wannamaker, you must be mistaken." Helga tried to sound genuinely surprised and concerned. "I do not understand why anyone would think I am a criminal."

He mentally noted her feigned confusion as he tested the microphone. Satisfied with the playback, he started the tape recorder. "This is just routine. Tell me about your activities between 1933 and 1945."

"That was so long ago—no one in Germany cares anymore, Mr. Wannamaker."

"Tell me what you can remember."

"Would you like coffee, Mr. Wannamaker? It will only take a minute."

"Mrs. Roth, sit down. As I said, this is just routine. Please describe your activities from 1933 until 1945."

He listened to her tell the same story he had heard before: she was young, was never a Nazi, did what everyone else did, never even left her hometown, etc. His mind started to wander until he heard her say something about Kraków. "Please repeat what you just said about Kraków, Mrs. Roth."

"I spent time in Kraków."

"How long were you there?"

"I do not remember. Is that important?"

Wannamaker shuffled through the file and found she was allegedly at Auschwitz from early 1942 until the end of the war. "You said earlier that you never left Nuremberg."

Helga kept her cool. "My boyfriend was stationed in Kraków, and I visited him occasionally. I did not leave Nuremberg permanently until I emigrated to the United States. I apologize for the confusion."

"What was the date of your last visit to Kraków to see your boyfriend?"

"I think it was July or August 1944."

"You were in Nuremburg after August 1944 until the end of the war?"

"Yes."

"Mrs. Roth, do you remember when the Allies started bombing Nuremberg?"

"The bombings started the day after I returned from my final trip to Kraków. I remember very clearly that I felt lucky my bag was still packed as I ran to a bomb shelter."

"That would have been July or August 1944?"

"That is correct."

"Mrs. Roth, you were nowhere near Nuremberg during the bombings."

Helga's face flushed with anger. "How dare you say that, Mr. Wannamaker. I remember very vividly watching the Allies destroy my beloved city."

"The Allies did not bomb Nuremberg until January 1945."

Helga did not answer.

"Of course, you could not have known that because you were in Poland."

She stayed silent.

"This would be much easier if—"

Helga pointed at him. "Young people do not appreciate what we accomplished for the Fatherland. We may not have gotten rid of every one of them, but I am proud to have done my part. Remember this, you spoiled little brat, it is the Jews. It is always the Jews."

Wannamaker pulled Helga out of her chair and handcuffed her wrists behind her back. "Helga Küster Roth, you are under arrest as a suspected Nazi war criminal."

ACKNOWLEDGMENTS

After seven years, *Mama's Ring* was completed with the help of many from around the world.

Thanks to Adelina Michaldo, Łukasz Lipiński and Piotr Setkiewicz at the Auschwitz-Birkenau Memorial and Museum in Oświęcim, Poland, for offering critical insight and taking me to places that few want to visit.

To Csaba Köves, who drove me through nine countries over thirty days and answered hundreds of questions along the way, thank you for your patience.

Thanks to The Illinois Holocaust Museum and Education Center, Virginia Holocaust Museum and the United States Holocaust Memorial Museum for your wonderful programs and exhibits.

Thanks to Eva Mozes Kor for allowing me to interview you at your museum, Candles Holocaust Museum and Education Center in Terre Haute, Indiana.

Thank you, Dr. Janice Spangler, Psy. D., for graciously sharing your knowledge of the psychology of evil with me.

To my dear friend of almost thirty years, Larry Mayer, thank you for your critical eye and for pushing me to finish the book.

Thank you, Mandy Adams, my wonderful stepdaughter, you inspire me to be kinder and more caring.

Above all, I thank my husband of twenty-seven years, Eric Adams. You have believed in me and in the book, especially when I did not.